To Bernice

Some light
Florida
reading!

By FRANK CERABINO

Illustrator: PAT CROWLEY
Editor: MARGARET McKENZIE
Designer: MARK BUZEK
Publishing liaison: LYNN KALBER

The Palm Beach Post
The Maple-Vail Book Manufacturing Group

The Maple-Vail Book Manufacturing Group
Willow Springs Lane
P.O. Box 2695
York, PA 17405

Printed in the United States of America

1st printing 2005

ISBN: 0-9705026-3-X

This book was printed by Maple-Vail Book Manufacturing Group.

Originally published in *The Palm Beach Post*
from March 6-27, 2005.

$8.95 U.S.

Preface

Pelican Park is not about life in a condo.

I thought I'd get that out of the way just in case you're one of those people who vaguely heard of a newspaper columnist writing serialized novels about condo living in Palm Beach County, Florida.

I am that columnist, and yes, *The Palm Beach Post*, has published three of my serialized novels about life in the fictional Shady Palms condominium in Boynton Beach.

But the book you are holding, *Pelican Park*, is something else. Call it my midlife crisis.

Instead of writing a fourth installment of *Shady Palms*, I got the urge to change generations and lifestyles, and trade in the condo board for a neighborhood association.

Pelican Park is about a fictional neighborhood in West Palm Beach, a community in the process of rebirth, much like the characters who fill it. The neighborhood, east of Interstate 95 and near Belvedere Road, isn't on any map. But you might feel you know it anyway.

The Post serialized *Pelican Park* in the Accent section of the newspaper, where this novel first appeared in daily installments during March 2005.

I am grateful for those of you who have already read it in that form, and for your kind encouragements to both publish the novel in book form and keep these characters alive in future tales from *Pelican Park*.

"My husband and I went away for five days, and I had my neighbors keep all the papers for me," a woman from Jupiter e-mailed me, while the story was being serialized. "On my return, I was like a little kid on Christmas, opening up all the papers and taking the Accent section out.

"I sat down with a glass of wine and read and read," she wrote. "I wish it didn't have to end."

Thanks to people like her, *Pelican Park* is still, for me, a neighborhood with a future. As I write this, I'm working on a sequel to this story.

But that's not your concern. Not right now. No, you just need to turn the page and congratulate yourself for getting into this real-estate deal on the ground floor.

1

A refugee from Boca

For Kathryn "Pinky" Hope, life took a new direction the morning her yoga instructor stayed home with a cold.

"No class?"

Pinky was unable to mask her disappointment as she stood at the reception desk of the Boca Raton gym with her rolled-up mat, Lady Athlete yoga outfit and a fresh dusting of makeup. This was, after all, practically her religion — the 90 minutes of the day that were just for her, a ritual that limbered her 42-year-old body, calmed her head and justified the day's inevitable chocolate.

"Isn't there a substitute yogi you can call?" she asked.

Some of the other yoga regulars were already heading for stationary bicycles, elliptical machines and treadmills. And for a moment, Pinky nearly did, too.

But she didn't, and it changed her life.

For when she got back in her Lexus and drove home, she got the second surprise of the morning, one that quickly outdid the yoga disappointment.

There weren't supposed to be any cars in the big paver-stone driveway, but there were two, and she instantly recognized both of them.

The green Chevy Suburban with the "Cosmo The Lawn King" magnetic placard on the driver's side door belonged to her husband, and the faded black Ford Taurus with the Broward County license plate was Celia's car.

Celia was the Brazilian woman who cleaned the house every Friday. But this was Tuesday.

Looking back on it, even then, Pinky hadn't imagined what was going on. Maybe Cosmo had forgotten his cellphone at home, and Celia had had a cancellation.

It wasn't until Pinky walked in the front door and heard them both upstairs in her bedroom that she realized that her marriage of 18 years was, in that moment, forever diminished.

At first, all she could do was rush out of the house and drive away as fast as possible. She was in such a hurry that she clipped a garbage can as she backed up, and hit her head on the headliner of the car's roof when she failed to slow down for the speed bump on the road leading out of her gated community.

By the time she reached I-95, she had to keep wiping her eyes with the back of her hand in order to see the road. She wasn't sure where she was going or what she was doing. She just needed to put distance between herself and her husband.

She raced up the interstate as if she were in a hurry to get somewhere, and by the time she got to Boynton Beach, she had started developing a plan, figuring out where that somewhere would be.

She would keep driving north, she told herself, maybe get all the way to the tip of Florida. Spend the night at the Ritz-Carlton on Amelia Island. Walk the beach, get a massage, eat breakfast in bed.

She fumbled for the cellphone in her purse and called her husband's work line. She took a deep breath, willing herself to sound calm and determined, rather than emotional.

But the sound of her husband's recorded voice made the anger and resentment build up.

"This is Cosmo The Lawn King. I can't come to the phone right now, but . . ."

By the time Pinky heard the beep, it was like a starting gun for her emotions.

"Cosmo! How could you? I know why you can't come to the phone right now!" she blurted out to his answering machine. "I know! I know! You . . . you . . ."

And then she started sobbing, right into the phone. A horn sounded as her car veered into another lane, and she dropped the cellphone. She got back in her lane, fished around on the floor and found it.

"As long as you're home today," she said, regaining some of her composure, "get Charlie and Luna at parent pickup this afternoon. And you may want to make them dinner, make sure they do their homework and put them to bed at a decent hour. And you also may want to get them up for school tomorrow morning, make their lunches, and drive them to school, and you may also want to keep doing that until I decide to come home, you dirty, rotten . . ."

Beep. The phone message clicked off.

She put her cellphone back in her purse, feeling worse now than before. She thought that telling him off would bring her some relief, but it only made her think about her two kids — their two kids. She couldn't run away from him without also running away from a boy and a girl who, like all children, needed to have a loving mother at home.

But she couldn't imagine sleeping in her own bed. She couldn't pretend that it was just another day in a long string of days that made up her otherwise uneventful, and seemingly harmonious, marriage.

She had to get away — didn't she?

There was no telling how far she would have gone if the low-fuel light hadn't caused her to pull off at Belvedere Road in West Palm Beach and look for a gas station.

She exited the highway going east and spotted the BP station on her right. She pulled up to a pump and went inside, buying $20 worth of gas. She must have looked a wreck.

"You OK?" the salesclerk asked.

"Hardly," Pinky said. "Where are the York Peppermint Patties?" she asked.

Standing next to the gas pump, taking the first bite of the chocolate-covered peppermint and staring into space, she became aware of a man on the sidewalk, across the street from the gas station. Old enough to be her father, he was sitting in a motorized wheelchair that was parked, not in the nearby shade, but under the already brutal May sun. She could see his reddened scalp under wispy white hair that reminded her of cirrus clouds, and she could see that his cotton shirt was soaked with sweat.

He sat there, waving at passing traffic, raising one hand off the arm of his wheelchair in a small gesture to acknowledge each passing vehicle.

A crazy man, Pinky concluded.

She got back in her car, put the air conditioning up high and started to pull out. The traffic on Belvedere Road caused her to wait there at the station, looking for a break in the line of cars.

If there hadn't been a lot of traffic that morning, she might not have given the man in the wheelchair a second glance. But when she did, she saw something she hadn't seen the first time. She saw the panic in his eyes, and she saw that his little wave wasn't a greeting but a feeble call for help.

She parked the car and walked across the street.

"You need to get out of the sun," Pinky said.

His hand was already on the lever that controlled the electric motor.

"Dead battery," he said to her, his voice a faint whisper.

She pushed the wheelchair into the shade and told him to hang on while she called for help.

"No!" he said, mustering as much energy as he could. "I can't afford the emergency room again. I just need to get home. Please, just take me home."

"You wait right here," she said, and ran back to her car.

She pulled up to the curb near the wheelchair.

He was sweaty and smelly, but he could put some weight on his legs, and he couldn't have weighed more than 120 pounds. So, with one of his arms around her shoulders and one of her arms around his waist, they were able to stagger together to the passenger seat of the Lexus.

"Here," she said, blasting the vents of the car's air conditioner on him.

The wheelchair was too heavy and bulky to put in her car. She just left it there.

"Don't worry," she said. "I'll deal with that later. Let's get you home."

First, though, she drove back to the gas station and got them both bottles of cold water.

"An angel sent you to me today," he told her after his first sip.

"Actually, it was a Brazilian."

He was 82, his name was Roger Billings, and he lived alone in Pelican Park, a neighborhood not far from where they were.

Today was his wife's birthday, and he had visited her grave site, but he had never attempted to go that far in his motorized wheelchair before.

He had gotten up before the sun rose, made the long trek to pay his respects and was nearly home again when his battery died. He had sat out there in the sun for more than an hour, amused at first, and then dismayed by all the people who seemed to notice him but never stopped.

"The only one was a homeless guy looking to rob me," the old man told Pinky.

He directed her to his home in Pelican Park. Despite her 20 years in Palm Beach County, Pinky had never been here before. She'd found almost no reason to leave Boca Raton, and to her, West Palm Beach was an airport location and nothing else.

"This used to be a nicer neighborhood," the old man said.

The houses, at least the ones that hadn't become neglected, were charming, Mediterranean-style stucco homes with hardwood floors, real chimneys and authentic charm — not the kind of manufactured faux-charm that was so prevalent in Boca's guard-gate communities.

A group of teenagers were in the middle of the street, clustered around a skateboard ramp. They stopped to watch Pinky drive by. A man in a grease-stained T-shirt was changing the oil of his car in his driveway, allowing the thick, brown liquid to drain in a stream that ran to the street. Farther down the block was a home with no fewer than two dozen lawn ornaments in the front yard and an exterior paint color that bordered on fuchsia.

Then they reached Roger Billings' home, which, like him, was small and unassuming. Pinky parked in his driveway and helped him inside.

"Sorry," he said feebly. "If I knew I was getting company . . ."

"That's OK. I'm the one with the mess at home," she said.

Then it hit her again, and without warning, she plopped down in one of his living-room chairs and began to cry.

"Oh my," he said. "What's wrong, dear?"

She told him, letting it all spill out, grateful now for the chance to say aloud all the things bubbling inside her. And he listened, really listened, and by the time she was finished, she felt stronger, no longer thinking she needed time to lick her wounds on Amelia Island.

"Life's a real doozy, ain't it?" the old man said.

She nodded, then thought of something and stood up.

"Your wheelchair!"

She jumped in the car and drove back to Belvedere Road, expecting to find the wheelchair on the sidewalk, where she had left it.

But when she got there, the wheelchair was gone.

2

In Hell's despair

Mark Stone sat on a milk crate, watching to see what would happen with the woman in the Lexus and the old man. He was glad someone had finally stopped to help the guy.

Stone had tried, but as he was learning, people arrive at troubling and often inaccurate conclusions when dealing with a homeless person.

"So, where are your flowers?" Stone had asked the old man in the wheelchair, after seeing him stranded on the sidewalk.

It was just a harmless greeting and a bit of idle curiosity. Stone lived much of his life these days on Belvedere Road, spending hour after hour going nowhere while a parade of humanity ebbed and flowed around him. So he noticed things others missed. He knew when snack cakes were delivered to the Smart Shop convenience store; when the No. 46 PalmTran bus was late; and when the freight trains would be rumbling by on the Florida East Coast tracks. He even knew how many rock-fill-loaded cars were on each train, because he made a point to count them.

Mark Stone knew the people who belonged on Belvedere: the strippers from the Kitten Club; the regulars at the Moose Lodge and at Roosters, the gay bar; and the customers at the Belvedere Valet Cleaners and Laundry. He knew when the Tulipan Bakery heated the ovens for the day, when the Greek brothers stopped working on cars at New Age Automotive, and when El Norteño ushered its last customer out the door in the wee hours of the morning. Living on the street made him an expert on its people and places, and gave him a sense of who belonged and who was out of place, someone just passing through.

And he was probably the only person in the city that morning to take notice, real notice, of Roger Billings when the old man made his pre-dawn trek along Belvedere Road with a bouquet of flowers in his lap.

Stone was sitting on his blue plastic milk crate on the northeast corner of Lake Avenue and Belvedere Road, wondering where this old man had come from and what had brought him on this journey. Stone watched Billings motor down the sidewalk of the quiet street, heading east over the train tracks and toward Dixie Highway.

And hours later, he noticed the man motoring back, and saw the moment when Billings' wheelchair stopped in the middle of the sidewalk. Stone watched Billings flail at the throttle of the chair, to no avail. And he noticed that the old man's mission, whatever it was, must have been completed because he no longer had the flowers in his lap.

But when Stone approached to help the stranded man, Billings took the question about his flowers as an overture to a robbery and bellowed for Stone to get away from him.

"I don't need no bum," the man said.

"You shouldn't be out in the sun like this," Stone said, as gently as possible, taking a few more steps toward the man. "I can . . ."

"Get away from me!" the old man said. "You stink."

Stone shrugged and walked back to the abandoned gas station, where he sat back down on his crate.

He could still see the old man from this spot, and Stone told himself that he'd keep an eye on him, and if nobody offered to help, he'd take another stab at getting the old guy out of the sun.

Stone was just about to do that when the woman in the Lexus stopped. She, like the old man, was a stranger to Belvedere, Stone noted.

"C'mon, help him," Stone said under his breath, as he watched the woman standing there, deciding what to do.

A part of Stone wanted to run across the street and offer his services. But a bigger part wanted to watch, to see if this prissy woman with her designer car and designer workout clothes would get herself soiled by dealing with the caustic old man.

So he sat and watched with great satisfaction as Pinky Hope dragged Roger Billings, with great effort, into her car. And Stone felt a pang of admiration for her as she leaned against the car to catch her breath after the job was done.

He whispered words, recalling them like a long-forgotten melody.

"Love seeketh not itself to please . . . Nor for itself hath any care . . . but for another gives its ease . . . and builds a Heaven in Hell's despair."

Poetry still came to him like this. It was a blessing, the flower that grew from the cracked sidewalk of his life, to still have poetry when so much had slipped between his fingers.

He felt grateful for this moment. For the woman in the Lexus. For recalling William Blake's poem. For a chance to experience something uplifting for a change.

He sat there for another half-hour, looking at the empty wheelchair and wondering whether the woman in the Lexus would come back for it. He hoped so.

But then something bad happened.

Ray-Ray, the 14-year-old neighborhood kid who never seemed to be in school anymore, came bouncing out of the BP station with his entourage, three boys, maybe a year younger than Ray-Ray, and they spotted the empty wheelchair.

Ray-Ray was a frequent tormenter of Stone's, rifling through the homeless man's pockets for change while he slept and taunting him while he was awake.

Stone made a point of staying away from the teenage thug. So his first instinct was to stay put and do nothing as he watched the four boys take turns pushing each other in the wheelchair, hooting and hollering, as they ran down the sidewalk with it.

He hoped they would tire of their new toy and just walk away. Instead, the posse apparently decided to keep the chair, bounding down the block, pushing Ray-Ray like a street king.

"Hey," Stone

said, approaching them. "Leave that alone. It's not yours."

He stepped in front of the chair, and the boys stopped pushing. Ray-Ray looked up at Stone with a malevolent smile.

"Yo, yo, yo, fellas. It's homeless dude."

"Shouldn't you be in school?"

"Shouldn't you take a bath?" Ray-Ray answered.

The others howled.

"You don't need that chair," Stone said. "It belongs to an old man."

Ray-Ray stood up. At first, Stone thought the boy was being reasonable. But then he saw the knife Ray-Ray had pulled from his pants pocket.

"Don't let me have to cut you."

Stone didn't need to be told twice. He stepped aside. Ray-Ray grinned and eased back into the wheelchair. Reaching in his pocket, he tossed a nickel onto the sidewalk at Stone's feet.

"I'm feeling charitable today. But next time you get in our way, we won't be so nice."

The boys moved down the sidewalk. Stone stared at the nickel for a moment, then kicked it before starting to walk back to his milk crate.

After taking a couple of steps, though, he stopped and turned, mustering the courage to trail the boys down the sidewalk.

As expected, they had stopped at the convenience store, leaving the wheelchair out front while they went inside to play video games. Stone looked at the empty chair and felt his heart beating rapidly under his tattered shirt.

He took a deep breath, and then without even turning to see if the boys had noticed, quickly wheeled the chair away. He rounded the corner, ran up Georgia Avenue, then stopped to see if he was being followed.

That's when he heard the brakes screech on the unmarked detective's car that had just happened to pull up to the intersection.

Stone tried to act nonchalant, but it was too late. The detective parked the car and climbed out.

Stone had had plenty of run-ins with the beat cops, the ones in uniform, and he had managed over the past few months to get to know them. The cops had reached a kind of understanding when they realized he was harmless. And Stone learned that the officers were content to let him be as long as he stayed out of people's way and didn't make a nuisance of himself by panhandling or scaring customers away from businesses.

So he'd become adept at blending into the weeds, disappearing behind the abandoned gas station at the corner of Lake and Belvedere. He had learned to become invisible, never doing anything as bold as this — running down the street with a valuable piece of equipment he didn't own.

"Whoa! Whoa!" the detective said, walking toward him. "What do we have here?"

Carl LaCerda was a property-crimes detective for the West Palm Beach Police Department. He had been cruising the neighborhoods near Belvedere, where there was always concern for more police presence, a concern that ricocheted from neighborhood crime watch volunteers, to City Hall, to his chief and eventually down to him — the end of the line.

"I was just returning it, officer," Stone stammered, avoiding eye contact.

"So it's not yours, then," the detective said. "Whose is it?"

"I . . . I don't know his name, but I know what he looks like."

"And where does he live?"

"I don't know."

"But you're running to return it to him?"

"I'm running to get away from some boys."

LaCerda pulled out his notebook.

"Name?"

"The older one goes by Ray-Ray, but . . ."

"Your name."

"Mark Stone."

"Where do you live, Mr. Stone?"

"At the moment, I guess I live locally."

"And where would that be?"

"Just . . . kind of around."

"I see. And where did you come from?"

"Oregon."

"And when will you be returning?"

"I don't know," Stone said.

"How about real soon?" the detective said.

"I . . . can't."

The detective looked hard at him now.

"That so? Care to tell me about it?"

"No. It's personal."

The detective smiled.

"Well, how about you pretend I'm Oprah, and you've just plopped down on my couch to talk and . . ."

"No," Stone said, softly now. "It's none of your business."

"But vagrants stealing wheelchairs is my business," the detective said.

"I didn't steal it," Stone said, looking into the man's eyes now.

"Got any family in the area, Mr. Stone?"

The question caught him off balance. He had to look away, staring at his feet now.

"Maybe," he said.

When he looked up, two squad cars were rolling toward them. LaCerda had apparently been waiting for this moment.

The detective and the two approaching officers began putting on rubber gloves. Stone knew there was nothing he could say now that would change whatever was about to occur.

So all he said was "Oh," as LaCerda began his recitation.

"You are under arrest, Mr. Stone. You have the right to remain silent . . ."

3
Last will and fundament

When Roger Billings died, only three people showed up for his funeral, and two of them didn't know who he was.

"This is creeping me out," 11-year-old Luna Hope told her mother.

Pinky sat in the second row of the empty church, looking over at the door at every sound, hoping somebody else would walk in.

"Put that away, Charlie," she told her 14-year-old son, who had been furiously fiddling with a Game Boy on his lap.

"Who is he, anyway?" he asked.

"I told you already. Roger Billings, a friend of mine."

"How come we don't know him, then?" Luna asked.

"I'm sure I mentioned him to you," Pinky said.

Actually, she wasn't sure at all. Her friendship with the old man had developed unexpectedly from the day she'd spotted him stranded in the wheelchair. It was an accidental friendship that had begun on what she would always think of as the worst day of her life.

Cosmo The Lawn King hadn't just dallied that morning with the Brazilian maid. He had spent years sleeping around behind Pinky's back, she had come to learn, making quick, midday stops at the homes of women who started out needing their lawns mowed and ended up being serviced indoors.

Cosmo hadn't confessed to any of it, but his former foreman, Julio Castro — a guy he fired for drinking on the job — was more than happy to supply Pinky's divorce lawyer with more details than she cared to hear.

"He would tell Castro he had to investigate an 'irrigation problem,' " the lawyer told Pinky. "That was the code he used to avoid being disturbed during these trysts. Castro said The Lawn King was off investigating irrigation problems as many as two, three times a week with a variety of women."

So that was it. She had been a fool, asleep through her own marriage, living with the incorrect impression that she and her husband were one of the lucky couples.

"Is Daddy coming today?" Luna asked at the church.

"No," Pinky said. "Daddy didn't know Mr. Billings."

During those first few weeks after discovering her husband's infidelity, Pinky found herself driving to West Palm Beach on a daily basis to see the old man.

At first, she convinced herself she was doing it for him. After all, he had no one in the world, and until he got his wheelchair back, he was helpless. So she shopped for him, tidied up his little house and kept him company during the middle of the day.

She fell into a routine of dropping the kids off at school, then driving to Pelican Park and spending the day with the old man until it was time to drive south again and pick up her children.

She gradually realized she was doing this for herself as much as for him. She couldn't face the people she knew anymore. She'd lived in Boca long enough to bump into people she knew wherever she went. And her pending divorce wasn't a secret.

That's because Cosmo The Lawn King had become a kitschy TV persona. He had built a high-volume lawn-care business with a parade of goofy television spots that featured him dancing with a weed whacker or doing something equally offbeat.

He was always dreaming up new commercials, which is why he came home one day with a Chihuahua, thinking of it more as a business prop than a family pet.

"It's good to have a gimmick dog," he explained. "Like that TV doctor on the news, who has Patrick, the little poodle. So now I got Gomez."

Gomez was a foul-tempered dog with too few teeth left in its head to contain his tongue, which tended to dangle out of one side of its mouth like a long, pink cigarette. The Chihuahua became a regular on the TV spots, and The Lawn King found it useful to take him along to meet new clients.

The commercials had made him a recognizable face, a faux

celebrity right up there with those two brothers who did pest control ads. So when his wife filed for divorce, it had reached the threshold of a newsworthy blurb in Jose Lambiet's column in *The Palm Beach Post*, appearing under the headline "Lawn King marriage mowed down by 'queen.' " As if it were her doing.

Pinky wanted to get away from the prying questions of the acquaintances she ran into at Publix, at the gym and at her kids' schools. She wanted to go someplace where nobody would look at her as Mrs. Lawn King and whisper to others about the latest dirt on her marriage.

So Roger Billings' little home in Pelican Park became an oasis for her, a place where everything she did would be greatly appreciated and everything she said would be listened to and yet not spread around.

The old man became her confidant, her friend and a kind of always-approving father figure. And she became his lifeline, in what would be the final year of his life. When he went into the hospital for the last time, she asked him, "Who should I call?"

He held her hand and said, "There's nobody. Nobody but you."

Now she regretted not having taken her kids to meet him. But she knew why she hadn't. They'd just have told their father or brought him into the conversation. In their innocence and conflicted loyalty to both their parents, they would disturb the little cocoon of comfort she shared with Roger Billings.

And so it was only now, at this brief, impersonal funeral service, that her children learned of the man who had been so important to their mother. The eulogy, or what passed for one, was delivered by a young priest who had obviously met Roger Billings only when summoned to administer last rites in the hospital.

It was so inadequate, and ultimately insulting, that Pinky found herself standing on shaky legs and blurting, "Wait!" when the priest finished his perfunctory remarks.

"I want to say something," she said.

The priest hesitated, as if trying to decide whether to allow it. Pinky plowed ahead, not waiting for a ruling.

"Roger Billings was a sweet, kind man. I only knew him when he was physically crippled. But while others may have seen a shriveled old man in a wheelchair, I saw him for what he really was. A wonderful mind, trapped in a failing body, a man who never lost his optimism or his will to live, despite the tough hand life dealt him. I will always . . ."

Pinky felt a tug on her dress and heard her daughter's voice.

"Mom," Luna whispered urgently. "You're crying."

Pinky waved her hands in the air and then sat down, as if her hand movements had sufficiently completed the rest of her thoughts.

The kids begged her for permission to wait in the car at the cemetery, and Pinky agreed, happy to say goodbye without a critical audience. When she got back to the car, Charlie and Luna were in the middle of one of their fights over control of the car radio.

She got in, shut the radio off and started driving. Charlie was the first to notice that they weren't heading back to I-95 and Boca Raton.

"Where are we going, Mom?"

"I want to take you someplace," Pinky said.

"Is it a mall?" Luna asked.

"No," Pinky said, nervous now about what she had to announce. "It's going to be our new home."

The kids knew about the pending divorce, and despite their parents' best efforts, they had been witnesses to some of the arguments during the past year. But they had no idea how it all would shake out: that their mother had yearned so much for a new start that she couldn't stand to stay in Boca. That she was ready to invent a new life for herself, which ultimately would mean a new life for them as well.

When Roger Billings was dying, he told Pinky he wanted her to have his home. She protested, but he told her it was already settled.

"You could sell it," he said. "Real estate in West Palm is going crazy."

At first, she thought that was just what she would do. But when her divorce lawyer discussed the pending financial disposition of their heavily mortgaged house, her husband's huge business debt and gambling losses — another surprise — she found herself saying aloud something she had barely given much thought.

"I don't want the house anymore," she had said. "And besides, I think the kids and I will be moving to West Palm Beach."

"Are you sure?" the lawyer had asked.

"Yes. I already have a place in mind."

But she hadn't broken the news to her children until now, on the day of Mr. Billings' funeral.

"But what about The Savages?" Charlie asked.

He had started playing electric guitar in a band with some neighborhood boys. It was, Pinky knew, the only thing her son seemed to care about.

"You can still play in the band," Pinky said. "It's not like we're moving to another state. It's only a half-hour away from Boca."

As she neared the neighborhood, Charlie and Luna grew silent, taking everything in.

"Here we are," Pinky said cheerfully, as they drove past a low stone wall that said "Pelican Park" on it. "This will be our new neighborhood."

Luna was the first to break the silence.

"Where's the guard gate?"

Pinky drove down the shaded streets, slowing down in front of the occasionally well-kept home and speeding past the fixer-uppers. She wished that a police helicopter wasn't overhead, making low sweeping circles over the neighborhood, and that as she turned a corner, they hadn't witnessed a K-9 officer releasing his dog into a home.

"Doesn't this neighborhood have a lot of character?" she asked.

"Lock the doors," Charlie said.

"We're going to be adventurers," Pinky said.

"Does Daddy know about this?" Luna asked.

Pinky stopped the car in front of Roger Billings' house. The lawn hadn't been mowed in weeks, and there was a soggy pile of newspapers on the walkway. But what she mostly saw was its charming front entryway, its terra-cotta barrel-tiled roof and a construction that real-estate people frequently refer to as "good bones."

"What do you think?" Pinky said.

"This is it?" Charlie said.

"Yuck," Luna added. "It's . . . old."

Pinky parked. Maybe they'd have to see the hardwood floors inside, the real fireplace, the mango tree in the back yard.

"Let's go in and have a look," she said, trying to sound as chipper as possible.

"Can't we just wait in the car, like at the cemetery?" Luna asked.

Neither kid made a move.

"No, you can't wait in the car," Pinky said. "This is going to be your home. Don't you want to see your new home?"

Luna started crying. Pinky focused her gaze on Charlie, hoping that her daughter's disposition might be altered as it sometimes was by her older brother's attitude. But Charlie just held his mother's gaze for a second before turning away, saying, "This place sucks."

"Suit yourself," Pinky said. "If you want to stay in the hot car alone, I won't stop you."

She got out and walked toward the front door. After a few steps, she heard two car doors opening and shutting. Pinky turned around and smiled at her children.

"That's better," she said.

The kids trudged toward her, and Pinky told herself that it would just take time for their mood adjustment. And she was right. It took only a few seconds for Luna's mood to radically change.

"Mom, turn around!" she shrieked, pointing down the driveway toward the back yard.

Pinky wheeled around to see what Luna was talking about.

A naked man was staring back at her, frozen for a moment, before turning and scrambling over the fence.

4
Drip dry

Detective Carl LaCerda knew from the start he didn't have the kind of evidence he needed to make the grand-theft charge stick against Mark Stone.

The detective figured that the lawyer at the State Attorney's Office would take one look at the case and decline to prosecute. There was, after all, no real evidence to suggest that the homeless man had planned to keep or sell the abandoned wheelchair.

But that was fine by LaCerda. Because he also knew that the homeless man couldn't afford to post bail, and chances were he'd done some other crimes on the street — maybe even that string of neighborhood car burglaries LaCerda was investigating.

So the cop locked him up and hoped to get lucky. At the very least, he'd scare the man enough so that when Stone did get out of jail, he'd make it a priority to relocate outside West Palm Beach city limits.

LaCerda was right about much of this: Stone didn't make bond, and the State Attorney's Office would, weeks later, decline to prosecute.

But he was wrong about Stone. He didn't confess to other crimes, and the last time the detective went to visit him in jail, Stone was no longer there.

"What's he doing in the hospital?" the detective asked.

His second week at the lockup, Stone became deathly ill, belatedly diagnosed with a case of staph, an infection that had been running rampant at the jail.

He spent six weeks on an intravenous drip. While he was in the medical ward, his case was officially dropped, a fact that never got duly recorded at the jail. So, when Stone had recovered, he wasn't set free but returned to the general population of the jail, where he remained for the next three months.

He might have been there longer had it not been for Santiago Klein, the newest member of the Palm Beach County Public Defender's Office. Fresh out of law school, Klein spent his first day at work looking over the impossibly long list of indigent clients he would be representing.

"How come there's no court date listed for this Stone guy?" he asked another lawyer in the office.

Klein didn't like the shrug he got for an answer. And he wasn't willing to assume that the old arrest date was probably a typo.

Five phone calls and 15 minutes later, Klein found out the horrible truth about Mark Stone: He had been the victim of a flimsy arrest, a jailhouse health epidemic and a lackadaisical paper trail that had kept him locked up without reason for the past six months.

Klein called for an emergency hearing the following morning and was waiting for Stone at noon when he walked away from the jail, a free man.

"Mr. Stone!" Klein yelled from the window of his Toyota Corolla. "Over here."

Stone walked over to the car, hesitating at first, because it was rarely good news when anybody wanted to see him. He half expected it would be Detective LaCerda, perhaps with another lecture about how he should leave town if he knew what was good for him.

But he smiled when he saw it was just that young lawyer, the one who had magically appeared out of thin air that morning to make right what Stone had been powerless to correct.

"Oh," he said. "It's you."

"Santiago Klein," the young man said, holding out his hand for a shake. "We didn't get much time to introduce ourselves in court."

Stone shook the young man's hand. "I want to thank you."

"And I want to apologize," Klein said. "C'mon, hop in the car. The least the state of Florida can do is buy you lunch."

When Stone was arrested, the jailers threw out the grubby clothes he had been wearing. So he had no clothes of his own anymore, except for the jailhouse jumpsuit on his back.

"First," Klein said, "we're going to have to get you some clothes. Lucky for you, we're the same size."

Klein drove past Belvedere Road, and Stone looked up and down the street, already noting changes in the past months.

"My new house," Klein said, pulling up to a small bungalow in Pelican Park.

Stone knew of Pelican Park. It wasn't far from Belvedere. But he made it a point to stay out of neighborhoods. Homeless people wandering neighborhoods were asking for trouble. The unwritten rule, he knew, was that he would be tolerated only as long as he hung to the commercial arteries.

"C'mon in," Klein said, standing outside the car. "You weren't planning to get dressed in the car, were you?"

Fifteen minutes later, they were at CityPlace — another bit of forbidden territory for Stone — sitting at a restaurant called Legal Seafood, Klein's idea of a joke.

Stone kept his head down, trying not to shovel the food down too fast.

"So, what are your plans?" the younger man asked.

Stone shrugged.

"You moving on?"

Stone shook his head.

"We need to find you a home," Klein said.

"No," Stone said, looking up now. "You've done more than enough for me, already."

"But you can't just go back to living on the street," Klein said. "You'll just end up back in jail."

"Mr. Klein, I . . ."

"Call me Santiago."

"Santiago, I need to go back to where I was."

"On Belvedere?"

Stone nodded.

"Can I ask you why?"

"I just do," Stone said.

The lawyer drummed his fork on the table.

"What did you do in Oregon?" Klein finally asked.

"I was a college professor."

"Really? What kind?"

"Poetry."

"Write your own?"

"I used to."

"What happened?"

"Things."

"How about family?"

Stone ignored the question.

"And you?" he asked. "Why are you a lawyer who spends time networking with the homeless when you could be using your education to more profitable ends?"

"My father, the late, great Harold Myron Klein, was an overeducated, professional lefty sympathizer who went to California to help the grape pickers. That's where he met my mom, a Chicana union organizer working with Cesar Chavez. And that's how I got to be Santiago Klein — the product of what can happen when cross-cultural activists take a break from their life's work.

"By the time I was 5 years old," Santiago said, "I knew more about Che Guevara, the march on Selma and the Triangle Shirtwaist Factory fire of 1911 than most adults ever know. I grew up with a protest sign in my hand instead of a baseball bat, and watched both my parents argue about whose turn it was to get arrested. My idea of teenage rebellion was to join the Young Republicans.

"But you know what they say, the apple never falls very far from the tree. So I couldn't see wasting a law degree by doing anything as banal as using it as a vehicle to get rich."

Stone finished the last bite of his crab cake.

"Does this mean we get to order dessert?" he asked the lawyer.

Over the next few months, Stone resumed his shadowy life on Belvedere Road, and Klein made a habit of looking for him and sometimes stopping to bring him clothes or food.

"I'd take you to a restaurant if you smelled a little better," Klein said during one visit.

"Yeah, I used to shower at the West Palm Beach Golf Course. The caretaker there would let me in early in the morning. But a couple of the members saw me, and now I can't go there anymore."

"So what do you do?"

"Salvation Army. Bathroom sinks at the city library. Rain."

That's when Klein told Stone about the outdoor shower in back of his house in Pelican Park.

"There's soap out there and everything," Klein said.

"I can't be walking through neighborhoods," Stone said.

The next time Klein visited Stone, he had an old bicycle with him.

"Bought it at a garage sale for 10 bucks," Klein said. "I know it isn't much, but now you got wheels. And no excuse."

Stone hid the bike in the alley behind the abandoned gas station on Belvedere and Lake, and the next morning, he pedaled away at first light, taking the quickest route to Pelican Park, basking in the sensation of speed and the wind blowing through his hair.

He got lost going through the neighborhood and nearly gave up searching for the house. If it weren't for Klein's Corolla, or more exactly the collection of bumper stickers and decals on the back — everything from "You Can't Hug Your Kids with Nuclear Arms" to "Boycott Taco Bell" and "Mean People Suck" — Stone would have pedaled past it.

He rode his bicycle down the driveway and parked it out of sight in the back yard. The shower, which had both hot and cold adjustments, was a real treat.

So much so, in fact, that Stone made a habit of stopping by three, sometimes four days a week. Klein, noticing the use of the shower, began leaving a razor and shaving cream for Stone. The yard was so secluded by the overgrown vegetation that no one in the adjacent houses could see into it. And the home that shared a backyard fence with the lawyer's was also screened by the trees and shrubs. It didn't seem to matter anyway, because the house behind Klein's was boarded up and apparently unoccupied.

So Stone began to stay longer and longer in the lawyer's back yard, taking time not only to wash his body, but to strip naked and wash his clothes in the shower, too. Then he'd hang them to drip dry while taking a nap in the hammock.

The only problem with that arrangement was that there was no direct sun there — not like the yard of the unoccupied house directly behind it.

So the day finally came when Stone decided he would speed things up by hopping the fence to hang up his wet clothes in the yard of the empty house.

He was asleep, naked in Klein's hammock, when he heard the sounds of car doors slamming and a woman's voice coming from the front yard of the empty house. In an instant, he was up, running across the yard and hopping over the fence to grab his clothes. He scooped them up with one hand, and was about to turn and run when he heard a girl scream for her mother. When he looked up, he saw this woman staring at him from the driveway.

Something about her face registered with him. He'd seen her before, but he couldn't remember where. He looked at her for a second, and she back at him. Then he turned and fled, climbing the fence, his heart racing.

5

Seeing Sindee

Pinky Hope tried not to panic in front of her kids.

"Mom," her daughter said. "That man was naked."

"Let's go back to Boca," her son said.

Pinky was fumbling for her cellphone, calling 911. She realized it was a bad sign to already be calling for police assistance in her new home before even walking in the door.

"Let's wait back in the car," she told the kids. "Just in case."

"Just in case what?" Luna said.

"In case there're more naked men in the house," Charlie said.

"Ewww," Luna said.

Pinky locked the doors and waited for the police to arrive.

A few minutes later, four squad cars were parked outside the house. The officers were polite and unfazed. They checked the perimeter of the property and walked inside, finding nothing. Then they all drove away, one by one, telling Pinky that a detective would follow up.

"This place smells," Luna said, walking from room to room.

"We're going to paint all the walls, tear out the carpets, throw out that couch," Pinky said. "You'll see. We're going to make it our very own home."

"Can I have black walls in my room?" Charlie asked.

"Whatever you want," Pinky said, already regretting the concession.

There was a knock on the door. The detective, Pinky thought.

But when she opened the door, she was surprised to see a younger woman in cut-off jeans shorts, a T-shirt tied off in a knot to reveal her flat, belly-button-ringed stomach and a broad, big-lipped smile framed by her too-blonde hair, which was tied back in a pony tail.

But what Pinky mostly noticed was an enormous pair of man-made breasts, the kind she only saw on women getting out of the passenger seats of cars being valet-parked at Boca Raton's Mizner Park.

"Howdy, neighbor," the woman said. "You OK? I saw all the cop cars."

"Oh, hello, yes," Pinky said. "Come on in."

The woman introduced herself as Cindy Swift, and it wouldn't be until later that Pinky would learn she spelled her first name "Sindee" — and, more important, why she spelled her name that way.

"My real name is actually Deloris Switzer," she confided as Pinky went through kitchen cabinets, grateful to find some coffee to brew. "Sindee is just my professional name. The 'dee' part is for Deloris. Get it?"

"What about the 'sin' part?" Pinky asked, happy now that both her children were poking around the house in other rooms.

"It's for business purposes," Sindee said. "I'm an Internet entrepreneur."

Pinky found a box of cookies that were stale but at least still edible.

"I have my own Web site," the younger woman said, pulling a card out of her pocket and handing it to Pinky.

In the upper left corner of the card was a photo of Sindee, taken from the cleavage up. She appeared to be in the middle of a soapy shower, and judging from the expression on her face, she was having the time of her life.

The card said, "You're Always Welcome at Sindee's House."

There was a Web address, too: *www.iseesultrysindee.com*

"Oh," Pinky said, after comprehending the message in the address.

"Nineteen-ninety-five a month," Sindee said. "Last month, I got my 300th subscriber. There's a big, wide world of pervs out there."

"What exactly do they pay for?" Pinky asked.

"To watch me in my house. I've got surveillance cameras in every room but the kitchen. That's my private space."

"Do you have to . . .?"

Sindee reached across the table and patted Pinky's arm.

"It's not what you think, hon," she said. "I'm no prostitute. I just walk around my house in a constant state of being underdressed."

"That's it?"

"And I take frequent showers. When I started taking extra showers, I noticed a big bump in subscriptions. I'm up to five showers a day."

"Maybe that nude guy in my back yard was looking for you," Pinky said.

"Nah. None of my clients have any idea where I live," Sindee said, "and hardly anyone in the neighborhood knows what's going on, either. I like it that way. I don't want the city breathing down my back."

"My lips are sealed," Pinky said.

"Besides, it's just temporary. I have big dreams. I'm saving up money to open up my own restaurant," Sindee said. "Hors d'oeuvres only. Finger food of my creation. All traveling on a conveyer belt in little plates, right in front of the long, curvy bar where diners will sit. Twenty-five dollars, fixed price. Stay as long as you like. Eat as much as you want. Just pull the plate off the belt as it goes by you. I've already picked out the name. Saucy Cindy's See Food Diner."

"Wow," Pinky said.

"And how about you?"

Pinky gave her a recap of recent events. She hadn't intended to go into great detail, but she was relieved now to talk to this strange new culinarily inclined exhibitionist of a neighbor. So she talked for the next 15 minutes, beginning from the day she missed yoga class and ending with seeing the naked man in the back yard that morning.

"And now what?" Sindee asked.

"I used to sell residential real estate," Pinky said. "I'm thinking maybe I'll get back into it."

"You could start right here in Pelican Park," Sindee said. "We can use somebody other than Marvin and his idiot son, Junior."

Pinky gave her a quizzical look.

"Mallow & Mallow," Sindee said. "They've got Pelican Park locked up. Go up and down the blocks, and just about every real-estate sign you see is a Mallow & Mallow. This is their turf, even though they live in El Cid."

Pinky had forgotten a lot about the business, but not the vicious competitive nature of residential real estate. She wondered whether she still had the needed killer instinct. Clearly, though, years of scrapping in Boca Raton's stores, parking lots and restaurants must be worth something.

"I'm not afraid of a little competition," Pinky heard herself saying.

"Atta girl," Sindee said. "We could use a neighborhood person selling real estate here."

And so that was it. She hadn't even told her children yet. But she had made her decision right there at the kitchen table in her new house. She was getting back in the real-estate game. Look out, Mallow & Mallow. A new secret agent had slipped under the radar.

"That lady was weird," Luna said later that day, after Sindee had returned home for her early afternoon shower.

"She's very sweet," Pinky said. "And she's going to make us dinner tonight, too. Isn't that nice?"

"I want to go home," Luna said.

"This is our home," Pinky said, going up to her daughter and stroking her hair. "We already talked about this."

"Yeah, but I didn't say yes," her daughter said. "Let's go back to Boca, and see Daddy and Gomez."

There was a knock on the front door, and Pinky was happy for the interruption. A man in black slacks, a short-sleeved dress shirt and tie was standing there, his unmarked police car parked in the drive.

"Detective LaCerda." he said, flipping her his badge, then appraising her in a less than circumspect way. "First name's Carl."

"Come in, detective," Pinky said, guiding him to the living room and wishing that her kids weren't hovering there to listen.

She told him about seeing the naked man in her back yard. The detective wrote down her name and jotted some notes as they spoke. Then, without looking up, he asked: "And how about Mr. Hope? Did he witness this?"

"Daddy's in Boca," Luna answered. "They're getting divorced."

Pinky glared at her daughter.

"Kids," the detective said, smiling at Pinky, as if they were old chums.

Pinky quickly brought the discussion back to business.

"Do you have any idea who this man in my yard might be?" she asked.

"Welcome to Pelican Park," the detective said.

"What's that supposed to mean?"

"You're not in Boca anymore, Pinky."

Did he just call her by her first name?

"Mrs. Hope," she said. Or at least almost said. But the moment she formed the rebuke in her mouth, her daughter started wailing, "I want to go back to Boca."

"Oh, hush, Luna," Pinky said, with more vitriol than she intended.

"Theft of personal property is a recurring problem in this neighborhood," the detective said.

Pinky looked at her children and said, "Maybe you should go back to exploring the house."

Neither of them moved.

"But this is the first peeping Tom report," the detective said.

"What's a peeping Tom?" Charlie asked.

"Charlie and Luna, I'm not telling you again," Pinky said. "You need to leave us alone here for a while."

She could see LaCerda smile and puff up his chest a little.

"Good idea," he said.

She gave the kids her laser-eye stare — the one that never failed to convey the idea that drastic punishment would follow if they didn't comply with her wishes.

She waited until she heard the sound of the television set in the other room before she spoke again.

"Won't you have a seat?"

"Gladly," LaCerda said, plopping next to her on the couch.

"I'm sorry," she said. "It's just that things are hard for them right now."

"I know," LaCerda said. "I went through a divorce a couple of years ago."

He opened the big three-ring binder he was holding on his lap and moved a little closer to her on the couch.

"Any familiar faces here?" he asked.

The binder was full of Polaroid snapshots of men's faces. Page after page, the faces stared back at her, faces that were sometimes full of contempt, but most of the time blank and expressionless.

"The usual suspects," LaCerda said.

"I don't see anybody here that —" Pinky started saying, before stopping at one photo.

"Him?"

"I don't know," she said.

But she did. Maybe it was the haunting eyes. Something about the man who looked at her for a brief moment had burned an impression.

"Who is he?" she asked.

"A homeless dirtbag who lives on Belvedere. He slipped away from me once before."

"What did he do?"

"He's a felon, Pinky. Can you help me put him away?"

"I . . . I don't know."

"I'll arrange a lineup," he said. "This will be great."

He patted her knee. "I'll be in touch."

Glancing down at his hand, Pinky thought, "You already are."

She escorted him to the door, and before he left, he took out a business card and scribbled a number on it.

"My home phone," he said. "In case there's anything you want to talk about. Anything at all."

"Oh," she said.

As soon as he walked out of the house, she double-locked the doors. When she turned around, her son was in the room, arms folded.

"That dude was hitting on you, Mom."

"Oh, Charlie, you have such an imagination."

She started to clean up the kitchen, but after putting the coffee cups in the sink, she felt a sudden, desperate need for escape. Her children were sulking on the living-room couch, little more than condemned prisoners already.

She yelled into the silence of the still house: "Who wants to go shopping at CityPlace?"

6

Members one of another

"Don't worry, they can't see you," Detective Carl LaCerda told her as he stood a little too close for comfort behind Pinky's right shoulder.

Her nose was practically touching the two-way glass. On the other side, five men stood in a bright room, responding to commands that LaCerda made through an intercom.

He had come unannounced that afternoon to her house in Pelican Park, interrupting her from filling the huge Dumpster in her driveway. She was taking great satisfaction in tearing her new home down to its basics — blank walls, bare floors and empty rooms.

The kids were still clinging to the notion that their Boca house wouldn't be sold and that their parents' marriage would be miraculously saved before the divorce became final. But in her head, Pinky had already moved to this little house in Pelican Park, which had become, like her life itself, something to improve through the process of removal.

She had been lugging a roll of old carpeting out the door when the detective's unmarked car pulled up. LaCerda smelled of cologne this time.

"Hiya, Pinky," he said, walking up to her.

"Mrs. Hope," she corrected, wiping the sweat from her brow.

She looked a mess, her hair in a bandanna, and her old T-shirt and shorts streaked with dirt. For once, though, she was happy to be less than presentable.

"The lineup is all ready to go," he said.

She hadn't given the naked man in her back yard another thought over the past few days.

"What lineup?"

"The sex offender," LaCerda said. "I picked him up this morning."

"Sex offender?"

"It was good you scared him off," the detective said, leaning close enough to gag her with his Aramis. "Last month, a woman was sexually assaulted in her home, just three blocks away. Still unsolved."

LaCerda didn't mention that the likely suspect was the woman's ex-boyfriend, a man who not only didn't share the height and weight characteristics of Mark Stone but who also happened to be of a different race. No, the detective had learned it was better to keep things simple.

"Of course, we can only charge your guy with lewd and lascivious conduct, a misdemeanor, because he never got the chance to do anything more."

Pinky suspected the detective of just trying to scare her.

"I just showed up that morning," she said. "He had no idea I was going to be there. It's not like he was stalking me."

"Not you, maybe. But how about one of your neighbors?"

Pinky thought of Sindee Swift, her voluptuous new neighbor who spent most of her day in a pay-per-view state of undress. And she nearly said something to LaCerda. But she liked Sindee, and the last thing she wanted was to get her in trouble with the police — or even worse, sic this wolfish detective on her.

Carl LaCerda was Pinky's problem, and she would have to deal with it.

"Give me five minutes to get cleaned up," she said.

So Pinky stopped working on her house to ride with LaCerda to the police department and to participate in the lineup he had arranged.

She knew instantly which of the five men to consider. The body language of the others was so obvious, the way they angled away from him. And he stood forlornly, looking down most of the time.

"What's his story?" Pinky asked. "The one on the right."

"You've identified Number 5 as the suspect," LaCerda said, in a voice that conveyed his satisfaction.

"No," Pinky said. "I just wondered about him."

"But that is him, right?"

"I don't know," Pinky said.

LaCerda barked into the intercom, "Number 5, please take three steps forward and look straight ahead."

The man was now just inches from Pinky's face, staring into the two-way glass. He was about her age, but looked older and defeated in a way that was silently shouted by the invisible weight on his shoulders and the sadness etched on his face.

She could see now that he could be a man capable of almost anything, a man who, like an abused animal, could have had his innate good nature pounded out by cruelty. Maybe the detective was right.

Looking at the man, Pinky felt herself shiver.

LaCerda put a hand on her shoulder.

"I could have him take off his clothes for you, Pinky."

"Mrs. Hope," she said, wheeling around and suddenly needing to get out of that room.

"That won't be necessary," she said, heading for the door. "That's him."

■

That night, Pinky went to her first Pelican Park Homeowners Association meeting. She wouldn't have gone if it hadn't been for Sindee, who, it turned out, was her block captain.

"C'mon, Pinky, it'll be fun," she said, showing up at her door wearing a T-shirt that said "Morality Police" and then in smaller letters, "Feet apart and spread 'em."

" 'Fun'?"

"OK, that was a lie, but you should come anyway."

Pinky had stayed away from the neighborhood association in her Boca Raton community. The group was always fretting about the "hatracking" of the ficus trees or algae in the entrance fountain. Pinky thought it all too mundane and contentious.

"If you're planning to sell real estate in Pelican Park, you'd better get jiggy with the PPHOA," Sindee said.

The group met in the home of a young gay couple on the next street. Craig Shelbourne was a paramedic with the city fire department, and his partner, Jake Fisher, was a waiter at Bradley's. They had bought a ramshackle house in Pelican Park five years ago and had made it charming.

Craig was president of the association and Jake its secretary.

"Jake isn't with us tonight," Craig said, exchanging pecks on the cheek with Sindee. "His mother has summoned him to Shady Palms for one of those ghastly condo clubhouse theatrical productions."

"How tragic," Sindee said.

"And who do we have here?" Craig asked, swiveling politely toward Pinky.

"This is Pinky Mulligan, our new neighbor and soon-to-be next real-estate mogul in Pelican Park."

Pinky blinked. She hadn't heard herself called by her maiden name in nearly 20 years.

The previous evening, Sindee had stopped by with a bottle of wine, which they ended up draining. As wine often does, it loosened

Pinky's tongue, and she found herself talking about how important it was to make a fresh start here in Pelican Park.

"I'm tired of being The Lawn Queen. I want to be me — whoever that turns out to be."

"I suggest a new name," Sindee said. "It worked for me. What's your maiden name?"

"Mulligan."

"You can be Pinky Mulligan again."

"But I'm not even divorced yet."

"I thought you said you were ready for a new start."

Pinky thought about it for a second, then smiled.

"Here's to Pinky Mulligan," Sindee said, holding up her wine glass in a toast. "Back and better than ever."

To Pinky, it was just wine talk. So she wasn't prepared the next night to be introduced as Pinky Mulligan to a room full of strangers. Sindee squeezed her arm and whispered, "Just go with it."

So she did, and just like that, over cheese and crackers and talk about traffic calming, she became another person, the person she used to be.

"Pinky, what do you think?" Craig asked her, trying to get her into a spirited discussion about her preference between speed humps and mini traffic circles.

"Oh," she said, long ago tuning out of the conversation, "I don't know."

She reached again for the bowl of chocolate-covered raisins, hoping it wasn't too obvious how many she had already eaten.

The discussion grew heated when the topic of a proposed Parade of Homes was brought up.

"Flamingo Park's been doing it for years," Craig said, "and we have some lovely homes here, and others that might become lovely if there were some incentive to show them off."

Sindee was shaking her head.

"Nobody's coming in my home," she said.

"It would be voluntary," Craig said. "And we'd select the homes."

"There's already a home tour going on in the neighborhood," squawked a voice from the speakerphone on the coffee table.

The voice belonged to "Uncle Sherman," a man nobody in the room had ever seen. He lived a couple blocks from Pinky, in a house mostly hidden by the overgrown vegetation in its front yard.

Sindee had filled her in before the meeting on the many wild theories in the neighborhood about Sherman Soloway: Former CIA agent? Reclusive millionaire investor? Defrocked Catholic priest? Retired war hero?

Only a few things were certain. He had a ham radio antenna on his roof, and he had always been a one-man Crime Watch Committee in Pelican Park. He never answered his door, and he used an answering machine to screen all incoming phone calls.

He requested any communications be written and handed through the mail slot on the front door of his house. Because he never ventured outside, he attended all association meetings only through speakerphones. He managed to stay abreast of police activities in the neighborhood with his devout attention to a police radio scanner, which he monitored round the clock. In preparation for every homeowners meeting, he would fax a handwritten log of all relevant police calls in the neighborhood since the previous meeting.

"A Parade of Homes is being conducted by burglars," Uncle Sherman said. "Perhaps Bishop Crumley needs to increase his sermons on the Eighth Commandment."

Sindee had told Pinky about Calvin Crumley, the pastor at The Holy Blood of the Everlasting Redeemer, the only church in Pelican Park. Crumley was a voice for his people, who saw the gradual gentrification of the neighborhood as a process that was squeezing them out.

Crumley, a large black man wearing a cleric's collar and a purple pillbox hat, had been sitting quietly for most of the meeting. But now he stood up to his full height and took a step toward the speakerphone.

"Wherefor putting away lying, speak every man truth with his neighbor; for we are members one of another," the bishop boomed. "Ephesians 4:25."

"Get your people in line, bishop," the speakerphone voice shouted back. "Uncle Sherman: 8:30 Monday night."

"Gentlemen," Craig said nervously, "let's not . . ."

But he was too late. Bishop Crumley walked over to the speakerphone and disconnected the line, creating a loud dial tone in the room.

"Welcome to our happy little family, Pinky," Crumley said, as he returned to his seat.

Pinky reached for another handful of chocolate raisins.

7

Kinky Pinky

Santiago Klein first noticed something was wrong when he discovered that the bar of soap in his backyard shower had gone untouched for the previous three days. Then, while getting gas at the BP on Belvedere Road, he looked up and down the street for Mark Stone and didn't see him.

But Klein didn't become too worried until days later, when Stone still hadn't turned up, and food the young lawyer had left for the homeless man had been ravaged by raccoons, with wrappers strewn all over the back yard.

The next day, Klein made a point of checking the booking logs at the Palm Beach County Jail, and that's how he discovered Stone had spent the past week behind bars.

He visited Stone at the jail that afternoon.

"Why didn't you call me, Mark?"

"You've done enough for me already."

"So what were you going to do? Plead guilty? Let the cops think you're some kind of stalker?"

"I shouldn't have left those clothes in your neighbor's yard," Stone said. "That was stupid of me. I thought the house was vacant."

"It was," Klein said. "She's new to the neighborhood."

Stone shook his head.

"I don't think so," he said. "I've seen her before."

"I'm more concerned by the fact that she saw you," Klein said. "She picked you out of a lineup, and she'll probably dial 911 every time she spots you in Pelican Park."

Klein stood up. "I'm going to work out a plea deal for you. Maybe I can get you out of here with time served. In the meantime, don't talk to any cops. I'm going to pay a visit to this Kathryn Hope woman to assure her that you aren't some maniac who's stalking her."

The lawyer was about to leave, but stopped. "And when I get you out," he said, "we're going to have a talk about finding you a suitable place to live."

"I can't, Santiago."

"Yes, you can. There are places. Programs. I have money. I can get you started."

"It's not the money, Santiago."

"Then what?"

Stone shrugged.

"The longer you live on the street, the longer stuff like this is going to happen," the lawyer said. "Let me help you, Mark."

"You can't."

"You need to get off Belvedere."

Stone closed his eyes for a moment, then opened them and smiled sadly at his friend.

"I can't."

Days later, Pinky woke to the sound of lawn mowers.

She had begun spending day and night at her new house in Pelican Park, which was gradually being reshaped in her image. She had already painted the inside walls and had paid a company to clean and seal the wooden floors. New furniture was arriving every day.

Last night had been the first she had spent in her new bed. With the kids on summer vacation from school, her sister in Connecticut had graciously suggested an extended visit from Charlie and Luna.

"I think you and Cosmo could use the time to sort out your marriage," Pinky's sister told her. "And Charlie and Luna are probably better off being elsewhere when you do."

The kids had jumped at the chance to visit their cousins and to get away from their warring parents. Pinky had tried to insulate them from the arguments, but her decision to move to Pelican Park had caused Cosmo to openly ridicule her in front of them.

At first, Pinky thought the mowers she heard were coming from her neighbor Sindee's yard. But then she heard the sound of a weed whacker just on the other side of her window, and somewhere in the mix of engine sounds, she heard a familiar voice.

She peeked between the blinds into the front yard. Sure enough, there was her husband, Cosmo The Lawn King, talking on a cellphone and leaning on his pickup truck, while a crew of his workers fanned all over her property.

"Oh, no, you don't," Pinky said to herself, quickly getting dressed and storming out of the house.

Gomez the Chihuahua spotted her before Cosmo did. The dog, looking out the driver's side window of the pickup, began barking furiously at her.

Cosmo looked up and continued his phone call with studied nonchalance, letting her stand there beside him for a minute before he hung up.

"Don't you have an 'irrigation problem' to attend to?" she asked.

He ignored the dig.

"So this is the palace, the reason you're willing to destroy the family," her soon-to-be ex-husband said. "I envisioned a bigger, nicer place."

"Cosmo Hope, you know damn well why we're getting divorced."

"Tell me, do you think the kids are going to like living here better than they do in Boca?"

"It's going to be an adjustment for all of us," she said. "And I'd appreciate it if you don't try to poison them with your negativity."

"Don't snap at me. I'm up here doing a good deed. When I got one look at your lawn, I thought, 'Oh, my God, this poor woman needs help.' "

"I didn't ask you to cut my lawn. I will pay you for today, and then don't come back. I intend to use another service."

"Yeah, I'll bet you're already sampling the services."

"On second thought, I'd like you and your crew to leave right now."

"I'd be afraid to live in a neighborhood like this," he said, ignoring her. "And I'm concerned about my children living here."

"Cosmo, don't try to screw up the life I'm making . . . because of you."

"Maybe we just need some counseling, baby."

"Let's start with castration and build from there."

"Is that any way to speak to the father of your children?"

"Go," she said. "I intend to let you be a good father to them, but leave me alone."

"It's not like you can just reinvent your life," he told her.

"I already have, Cosmo," she said, reaching into her pocket and pulling out one of her new business cards.

" 'Pinky Mulligan'?"

"The new me," she said.

While they were busy arguing, Pinky and The Lawn King hadn't noticed the arrival of a Toyota Corolla, which was now parked behind Cosmo's truck.

"Excuse me," interrupted Santiago Klein. "Did I come at a bad time?"

"Yes," The Lawn King told him.

"No," Pinky said.

Klein looked confused.

"I'm Pinky," she said, extending her hand. "I own this house."

"Pinky Mulligan?" Klein said.

"Yes," Pinky said, happy that the young man knew her business name.

"The new real-estate person in the neighborhood, right?" Klein said. "I got your flier."

"Oh, isn't this just fascinating!" The Lawn King said.

Klein looked at him for a moment, sensing his hostility, then turned back to Pinky.

"I'm Santiago Klein," he said. "I live right behind you."

"I'm Cosmo The Lawn King," Cosmo said, holding out his hand for a shake. "But then again, I'm sure you already know that."

Santiago shook Cosmo's hand and shrugged.

"There's ole Gomez, in the truck," Cosmo said, pointing at the Chihuahua.

"Gomez?"

"I don't think Mr. Klein has had the pleasure of watching your TV commercials," Pinky said.

"Actually, I don't have a TV," Klein said.

"Don't have a TV?" Cosmo said. "That's understandable in this neighborhood. Somebody probably stole it."

"No, I just don't choose to spend my time that way."

"That's very admirable," Pinky said, adding, "Santiago" for a personal touch.

"Sounds un-American to me," Cosmo muttered. "By the way, I'm her husband. And her last name is still Hope, not Mulligan."

"Estranged, soon-to-be former husband," Pinky said. "And he was just leaving."

"Maybe I ought to come back another time," Klein said.

"That would be great," Pinky said.

"Now's as good a time as any to say what's on your mind," Cosmo said.

"I represent the man you identified in the police lineup," Klein told Pinky.

"Oh," Pinky said.

"Police lineup?" Cosmo bellowed. "What police lineup?"

"I'm an attorney with the Public Defender's Office, and I can assure you that there was nothing lewd and lascivious about my client's actions in your back yard."

"Whoa, whoa, whoa!" The Lawn King was yelling.

Pinky reached out and touched Klein's arm.

"Santiago, could we talk about it tonight, maybe over dinner on Clematis Street?" she said. "My treat."

"I want to hear more about your client and what he did in my wife's back yard," Cosmo said.

"It's none of your business," Pinky said.

"I'll . . . see you later then," Klein said.

"Pick me up at 7?"

"Sure, sure," Klein said, flustered now, as he turned to The Lawn King. "Nice to meet you."

"Get a television, weirdo."

Cosmo turned to Pinky, who had her arms crossed now, and an edge in her voice that was new.

"This conversation is over," she said. "Get you and your crew off my property. Pronto."

"I'm billing you for a mow-blow-and-go," Cosmo said over his shoulder, as he followed Klein down the drive.

Both men got in their cars and drove in opposite directions.

Aware that neighbors might be watching, Pinky willed herself to stand there, to pretend she was unaffected by it all. A moment later, Sindee came bounding out her front door, coffee in hand.

"I saw you out here with your husband, and I didn't want to interfere," Sindee said. "But who was that other guy you were talking to?"

"A neighbor," Pinky said.

"Really?" Sindee said. "He's kind of cute."

"We're having dinner tonight."

"You go, girl."

"No, it's nothing like that."

"That's what they all say."

"He just wants me to cooperate."

"Sounds kinky."

"Kinky Pinky, that's me."

She smiled at Sindee, but the corners of her eyes were already moist with the beginning of tears.

8

Honest food

That night, Pinky tried on half her wardrobe before settling on a simple Ann Taylor outfit of black slacks with a white silk sleeveless top.

"Not inviting enough," Sindee said, as she sat on Pinky's bed.

"I'm not trying to be inviting."

"Why not? He's cute."

"This isn't a date," Pinky said.

"That's not what Dr. Laura would say," Sindee said, rummaging through Pinky's closet until she found a blouse with a plunging neckline.

"How about this little number?" she said, holding it up to Pinky.

"Isn't it time for you to take another shower?"

In 18 years of marriage, Pinky had never cheated on her husband, even during the months of its unraveling. So when Santiago Klein pulled in her driveway that night, she felt as if she were crossing the border into a long-forgotten land. Part of her felt like a teenager again, with the rekindling of those long-dormant sensations of expectation and surprise.

And even though she told herself that this was nothing, just a neighborly chat, she felt almost dizzy. The tiny, invisible hairs on her arms stood up, and she reached for her sweater even though it was still in the 80s outside.

"I'm going to want a full report," Sindee said, before letting herself out the back way.

Pinky sat down in her living room, the peach-colored walls still drying from the coat of paint she had applied that afternoon. She waited until she heard a knock on the front door.

"I hear that new French brasserie on Clematis is good," Pinky said, as she settled into Santiago's Corolla, once he had put all the Amnesty International leaflets in the back seat.

"I'm sure it is," Santiago said. "But I'm not in the mood for a fancy restaurant. Is that OK?"

"Oh," Pinky said.

"It's just that, I don't know, sometimes when I eat in one of those nice restaurants with sidewalk tables, I feel like such a bourgeois pig — one of those wasteful, over-consuming Americans that the rest of the world loves to hate."

"Oh," Pinky said again. "I just feel . . . nice."

"There's a little place on Belvedere I like."

"Santiago, if it's the money, please, don't worry. I said tonight would be my treat."

"I think you'll like this place," he told her. "It's honest food."

"What's honest food?"

"Food that survives on its own merit — you know, without all the presentation, the dimmed lighting and the drizzled sauces. Food that stands up on its own. The meal equivalent to Neil Young."

She must have had a strange expression on her face, because he stopped mid-sentence and asked, "Am I confusing you?"

"Absolutely not," she said, even though she had the mistaken notion that Neil Young was an astronaut.

He pulled into a shopping center with a Winn-Dixie supermarket at one end and a McDonald's at the other. At first, Pinky thought he was taking her to the Subway sandwich shop, which was the only restaurant she saw in the long strip of stores next to the supermarket.

"I think I have a coupon at home," she said.

He laughed.

"Pinky Mulligan, you're a riot."

It was strange hearing her old name again. Strange to be in another man's car, and strange walking into Taqueria Guerrero, which had iron bars on the windows and fliers for Mexican bands taped to the door.

She felt like a fool now, for taking an hour to get dressed for this: some Third World diner full of laborers — many still wearing their sweat-stained ball caps — and large families who packed around the small tables, while a jukebox in the corner blasted country music from another country.

"This OK?" Santiago asked, pointing to a table near two men who were sipping beer from long-necked bottles and who hadn't bothered to brush the grass clippings from their shirts.

"Fine," Pinky said, taking the seat that faced away from them and reaching for the menu, which was in Spanish.

A part of her wanted to say right then that her husband, louse that he was, had taken her to La Vieille Maison on every anniversary and that they had carefully read restaurant reviews and took great delight in eating what this young public defender might call dishonest food — or whatever he'd call food at a proper restaurant.

Instead, she just sat there silently, staring at a menu she didn't understand, while Santiago chitchatted in Spanish with a plump, young waitress who seemed to know him.

When he finally turned his attention back to Pinky, he said, "So, what'll it be?"

She had already given up on the menu.

"Just order me something honest," she said.

She was hoping for a bottle of Chardonnay but settled for a Dos Equis beer. And by the time the food arrived, she had already downed a second beer and was ordering a third.

The food was actually quite good, and once she blocked out the jukebox and tried not to notice how sticky the table was, she was able to relax.

The beer helped, too, and she found herself half listening to this man, who had to be a good 10 years younger and half marveling that a year ago she would never have imagined any of this.

"See that tomato in that salsa?" he said. "Have you ever wondered what it took to get that tomato there in that bowl?"

She hadn't. But he had. He launched into a 20-minute discourse on the exploitation of farm labor, guiding her from the slum conditions in Guatemala to the farms in Florida, where workers are treated not much better than slaves.

He transitioned from labor politics to a condemnation of America's immigration policy. Pinky ate quietly, imagining the evening she thought she was going to have: sipping wine at a sidewalk table at a fine restaurant, while talking about her life to a man who hadn't heard it all before and would be intent on listening.

"You've been quiet, Pinky," Santiago finally said, after wrapping up his analysis of the North American Free Trade Agreement.

"Listening," she lied.

She felt foolish now, and by the time Santiago Klein started talking about Mark Stone, the naked man in her back yard, she had, for the first time, some doubts about her new life and a yearning for what she had back in Boca.

She missed her yoga class, her sushi lunches, her leisurely afternoons at the Town Center Mall. She missed her married girlfriends and their girls-night-out little evenings, when they would sit cross-legged in one of their living rooms, making each other laugh to the bladder-control threshold.

She didn't care about where her tomatoes came from, or about minimum-mandatory sentencing, or about the plight of a homeless man who was naked in her back yard for so-called innocent reasons.

The beer swirled with the jukebox accordion, and she couldn't decide whether she wanted to take off her shoes and dance, or put her head down and cry. Wasn't she entitled, after all, to venting her own midlife crisis?

"Tell me something, Santiago," she said, interrupting him. "Do you find me attractive?"

The young lawyer reddened and put down his fork.

"Be honest," she said. "I mean, I know you're younger than me, and maybe I'm not your type. But, I just need to know for myself. Because, well, I've been out of the game so long . . ."

He was staring at her now, not chewing, his mouth still full of food.

"I know I've got to lose 5, 10 pounds," she said. "That's a given."

The jukebox suddenly went quiet. Santiago swallowed.

"Pinky," he said. "You're beautiful."

She looked at him then and didn't see an ounce of fraud in his eyes. And at that moment, he had recovered all the ground he had lost so far that evening.

The jukebox roared to life again.

"Let's get out of here," she said, "and find some chocolate."

They ate gelato at CityPlace, sitting out by the big fountain, watching it come to life and then go dormant again.

By the time he was driving her back to her home, she had told herself that anything was possible. She kicked off her shoes in the car and relaxed into her seat, closing her eyes.

He pulled into her driveway and turned off the car's engine.

How long had it been since she had been held and kissed? She knew all along, from the time she started getting dressed, that this was the moment she had played over and over in her head.

Would he lean over and make a motion to kiss her? And what would she do? Would she offer a cheek? Or would she boldly kiss him on the lips and invite him inside?

She sat in the parked car, making no motion to open the door.

"Pinky," he said, and she could sense the hesitation in his voice. He reached over and held her hand.

"I know this is kind of forward of me," he said.

She turned in her seat, parting her lips slightly in anticipation.

"Yes?" she said, her voice nothing but an invitation.

"I'm not very good at this sort of thing," he said.

"What sort of thing?" she said, her voice a whisper.

"You know."

"Do you want to come inside, Santiago?"

"No, that's OK. This is as good a place as any to get it out."

"Oh, my," she said. "It's not necessary — my kids are at my sister's home in Connecticut."

"I don't want you to feel pressured," Klein said. "Because I like you and wouldn't want anything to jeopardize that."

"That's sweet of you," she said, leaning closer to him.

"It's just that I hope you'll go along."

"I guess you're about to find out," she said, closing her eyes and moving her lips a few inches from his face.

Her heart beat rapidly now, her lips waiting for that first bit of contact.

She could hear him turning sideways in his seat to face her.

"OK, here goes," he said. "Mark Stone can mow your lawn."

She opened her eyes and saw him there in the darkness, with a goofy smile on his face.

"What do you think?" he asked.

"What?"

"It's a perfect solution," he said. "You need your grass cut, and he could use the work."

Pinky sat back in her seat and reached into her purse for the house keys.

"I've got to go."

"So what do you think?" he asked, as she opened the car door and stepped out.

"I don't want some homeless guy hanging around," she said, walking rapidly toward the house.

Klein followed her up the walkway.

"I'll pay for the first few times," Klein said. "You don't have to do a thing. If you don't want him to continue, just let me know."

She put the key in the door, opened it and spoke without turning around.

"Thanks for a lovely evening."

She closed the door behind her, not moving until she heard his car drive away.

The ringing telephone in the house startled her. Sindee, she figured, was calling for a recap of the evening.

But when Pinky answered the phone, she heard the small, ragged voice of her daughter, calling from Connecticut.

"Mommy?"

"Honey? What's wrong? You OK?"

"I miss . . . everything," Luna said.

"I do, too," Pinky said, sagging to the floor and leaning back against the fresh paint.

9

Homecoming

When Charlie Hope and his sister, Luna, flew back to Florida, a flight attendant walked them to their seats on the plane.

"And where do you live?" she asked.

"Boca," Luna answered.

"Not anymore, stupid," Charlie said, not meaning to sound so mean but unable to control himself.

His sister was getting on his nerves.

"Oh, yeah. I forgot. West Palm Beach," the girl said. "We're going to a new school this year."

"Isn't that exciting!" the flight attendant gushed, looking at Charlie with a fake smile.

"Not really," the boy said.

If it were up to him, Charlie would have just stayed in Connecticut at his cousins' house. They had PlayStation 2 and a cool hill in their neighborhood, and there was a little refrigerator downstairs kept full of soda.

His aunt and uncle seemed happy to have him and Luna for the summer, and it wasn't like they didn't have the room. The house had a basement and a second floor and an extra guest bedroom that was being used as an office.

He had nurtured a secret hope all summer that his aunt and uncle would sit him down and ask if he wouldn't rather just live with them indefinitely while his mother and father sorted out their "marital difficulties," as his Aunt Nora liked to say.

And why not? Charlie had come to believe that there was nothing worth returning to Florida for. The Savages had found another guitar player over the summer, and he was going to be an eighth-grader in a school full of strangers.

He could just go to eighth grade in Connecticut. Then maybe by the time he was ready for high school, his parents would come to their senses, and they'd be back together again in Boca, and he could start at Spanish River High School with all his old friends.

That was Charlie's unspoken dream, and every night, he sat across the dinner table from his Aunt Nora, waiting for her to ask him. And he kept rehearsing how he would pretend to think about it, before saying, "Yes, let's give it a try."

His sister, on the other hand, had wanted to go back to Florida practically from the moment she arrived. She was always asking if she could call her mother or father and was now, on their return trip, the happiest she had been in two months.

"It's not like we're even a family anymore," he'd told her one night in Connecticut, after she had one of her crying spells.

"We are, too," she had said. "You'll see."

But he didn't see. When the plane landed in West Palm Beach, their two parents weren't standing together in the airport to greet them.

It was just their father, wearing his Cosmo The Lawn King work shirt.

"Where's Mom?" Luna asked immediately.

"I'm here," her father said.

"I know, but why isn't Mom here?" Luna asked.

"Because they hate each other, dummy," Charlie said.

Cosmo snorted, mock-punching his son on the arm.

"Well, that's not entirely true, sport," he said. "I don't hate your mother."

They walked to the parking garage, where Gomez the Chihuahua barked like a maniac when he saw them and then jumped from lap to lap as they drove away from the airport.

"Are we going home?" Luna asked.

"How 'bout we get ourselves some lunch?" Cosmo said. "I think I can let the fellas work a couple of hours without me."

"I'm not hungry," Charlie said.

"Well, then you can watch me eat," Cosmo said. "So, school starts tomorrow?"

"Are we going home?" Luna asked again.

Lunch at the restaurant was a disaster. Neither Charlie nor his sister ate very much. And in the middle of it, some woman with big, poofy hair and too much perfume arrived, putting a hand on Cosmo's shoulder as she slid into the booth.

"This must be the famous Charlie and Luna," she said.

"Kids, this is Deirdre."

"Is she your girlfriend?" Luna asked.

Charlie pretended to study his french fries.

"Deirdre is a good friend," Cosmo said, putting his hand on top of hers.

Charlie looked up, noticing for the first time that his father no longer wore his wedding band.

"Excuse me, I gotta use the bathroom," the boy said.

He locked himself in a stall and sat there for 15 minutes. Finally, his father walked in, washed his hands and announced, "C'mon, it's time to go" before walking out.

When Charlie emerged from the bathroom, his father and Luna were standing at the cash register, and Deirdre was gone.

"There are just some things we're going to have to get used to," Cosmo said, as they got back in his truck.

Neither child said a word. They rode silently to Pelican Park, the only sound coming from the asthmatic panting of Gomez.

Charlie was surprised at how much his mother had transformed the house from the day he first saw it after that creepy funeral service. He walked through the place, marveling at the shiny wooden floors, the new furniture and the unfamiliar art on the walls.

Almost everything about the place was different, with hardly anything, except for an occasional appliance, coming from their old house in Boca. It was as if his mother had used the summer to completely remake her life, and Charlie saw it now for the first time.

She hugged him tightly when he walked in with his father and sister, and she told him that she loved him and missed him. But he pulled away quickly, unwilling to return her affection, as his sister had so readily done.

"Come with me," his mother said, taking his hand and pulling him through the house. "I want to show you something."

She walked him back toward his bedroom, and he saw the beaded curtain in the doorway. He had always asked for a beaded curtain, and she had always said, "No," claiming that his fascination with '60s counterculture décor was incompatible with her sense of style.

"Go ahead," she told him. "Have a look."

She stepped back now, as Charlie marveled at the colorful rows of hanging beads before parting them between his fingers and listening to their sound — like plastic rainfall.

But what he saw on the other side of the curtain was what made him say, "Wow." She had painted the walls black. And she had put up posters of Jimi Hendrix and Jim Morrison. And on his dresser, a lava lamp percolated blue blobs in slow motion. She had bought a stand for his Fender Stratocaster, and it sat there, propped up in a corner of the room.

He sat on his bed, taking it all in.

"So, you like it?" she asked.

He stood up to hug her, but in that moment, the beaded curtain parted, and his father was standing between them, with a look of obvious dismay.

"Doper room," he said. "Whose idea was this?"

Charlie sat back down on the bed.

"What happened to that Shaq poster I got you, and the baseball signed by the Marlins?"

Charlie shrugged as his sister pushed through the beaded curtain. Luna was so wound up she didn't even take in her surroundings.

"The naked man!" she screamed. "He's . . . mowing our lawn!"

Mark Stone was confused by the sight of the lawn-maintenance truck in front of the house. Maybe he had misheard. But he could swear that Santiago Klein had told him that this was part of the deal: He would have to mow the lawn here.

"It will be good for you," Klein had said, after springing Stone from the county jail. "It will put some money in your pocket."

"Where will I get the mower?" Stone had asked.

Klein had that part arranged, too.

Stone wanted to tell the young lawyer that his good intentions were bound to cause trouble. That homeowners didn't want to see a homeless man in their neighborhood, even if he was working.

But instead, Stone just nodded and said, "Thank you," to the only person in the world who seemed to care about him.

He had found the mower gassed up and ready to go in the garage of Klein's next-door neighbor, just as the lawyer had said. And as he walked it over to the next block, he felt purposeful — an unfamiliar, stirring state of being for a person who had come to spend day after day with no expectation of accomplishment.

The small wheels of the lawn mower clattered on the street, and another bit of Blake's poetry floated up to him, like an answer from a

Magic 8-Ball.

"He who binds himself to a joy," he said. *"Does the winged life destroy . . . But he who kisses the joy as it flies . . . Lives in eternity's sun rise."*

He was hoping the house would be empty, so he was disappointed to find not only a car in the driveway but also a lawn-maintenance truck out front.

He nearly turned around. But he didn't want to disappoint Santiago. So he fired up the lawn mower and began cutting the front yard.

He had done only a few rows when he was aware of a man standing in front of the house, with a boy and a girl next to him.

Stone cut the engine, and a toothless Chihuahua darted from between the man's legs. Before Stone knew it, the dog was nipping at his pants.

"Gomez!" the man said. "Get back here."

Cosmo The Lawn King picked up his dog and regarded Stone.

"Where's the rest of your equipment?"

"This is it," Stone said.

"What about the edging, the trimming around the sprinkler heads, the blowing?"

Stone shrugged.

"What do you intend to do with the clippings?" Cosmo asked, pointing at the mower bag, which was nearly full.

Stone hadn't thought of that.

"I don't believe it!" Cosmo said. "You don't even have a lousy bag, do you?"

"Cosmo!"

It was the woman, and she was standing by the front door, apparently not willing to come any closer.

"This is none of your business, Cosmo," she said.

Cosmo turned to her.

"Who is this guy?" he asked, as if Stone weren't even there. "He looks like a street person."

"Kids, go inside," the woman said.

But the boy and girl just stood there.

"The last time he was here, he had no clothes on," the girl said.

"Luna, I said go inside."

Cosmo took a step toward Stone.

"What's going on here?"

"Cosmo, this is none of your business!" the woman said again, still keeping her distance.

Stone stared at the ground.

"Sir, why don't you come back another time?" he heard the woman say.

"Sir?" Cosmo said. "I don't believe this. I don't care what you do with your life, Pinky. But I care about what you do with our children, and as a lawn-care professional, it's not in my nature to see your lawn-care needs be turned over to . . . this."

But when Cosmo turned back, Stone was already walking away, dragging the mower with its bag full of clippings down the street.

10

Insignificant others?

Pinky's second homeowners association meeting, like the first one, devolved into some less-than-neighborly bickering.

"I just think we ought to have a motto, something to put on the lamppost signs that explains who we are to the world," Craig Shelbourne said.

Sindee rolled her eyes.

"Like, 'Come for the speed humps — stay for the traffic circles,' " Craig's partner, Jake Fisher, said.

"No, I'm serious," Craig said. "How about 'West Palm's next great neighborhood'?"

Uncle Sherman's speakerphone erupted. "How about, 'Lock all valuables. Thieves on the loose'?"

Uncle Sherman had already lectured the gathering on the steady stream of car break-ins and open-garage thievery. He ended his wrap-up by saying, "Those black kids on the north end are just taking us to the cleaners."

This created an immediate response from Bishop Crumley.

"Don't start condemning people before you have the facts," he thundered. "Your assumptions are racist."

"Now, now," Craig had said. "Let's keep this on a positive note."

But he couldn't steer the conversation back.

"The bishop's right," said Marjorie Wakefield.

The retired bookkeeper, who lived alone, attended meetings but usually left without saying a word. Now, just the sound of her voice made everyone turn to listen. She seemed flustered by the attention, but she continued.

"There's a homeless man," she said. "I've seen him several times. I don't know what he's doing here. I used to just see him on Belvedere, but now he's in the neighborhood."

Pinky looked away, hoping nobody would turn to her.

"That's right," Bishop Crumley said. "This is an open neighborhood. People come and go all day long. To blame everything on a few African-American teenagers who happen to live here is just plain wrong."

The meeting was also Pinky's first opportunity to meet Marvin Mallow, a dour, silver-haired man with sharp creases in his pants and even sharper looks at Pinky, eyeing her with the disdain he reserved for competitors.

She didn't get a chance to talk to him until the meeting was over, approaching him as he scrutinized a cheese tray without taking any.

"Hi, Mr. Mallow," she said. "I'm Pinky Mulligan."

"Yes, I know who you are," he said. "You're in the old Billings house."

Pinky handed him one of her new business cards. Mallow handled it like anthrax.

"I'm just getting started again in real estate," she said.

"So I've heard," Mallow said, handing the card back to her.

"You can keep it," she said.

But he pressed it back into her hand.

"No, thanks," he said. "So, is this some kind of a hobby with you, Mrs. Mulligan?"

"Hardly," she said, looking hard at him now, the niceties gone. "Call me Pinky."

He shook his head.

"I've been selling homes in Pelican Park for 40 years," he said. "My calendar hangs in every kitchen. My jar grip is in every drawer. The little flags that fly on every lawn on the Fourth of July are courtesy of Mallow & Mallow."

Pinky smiled thinly.

"Not every home, Mr. Mallow," she said. "In case you haven't noticed, I've already got several listings in the neighborhood."

"You've got precisely two," Mallow said. "A pittance."

"A start," Pinky said.

He patted her on the shoulder in a dismissive way.

"You're not the first, you know," he said. "When you're finished with your little exercise in futility, call me. Maybe I could use an extra associate."

"Dream on," Pinky said, sticking her business card in his jacket pocket and walking away.

By the end of the meeting, Pinky had a headache and a position on the newly created Pelican Park Motto Committee, which consisted of her and Jake.

"So where are we going to have our first meeting?" Jake said. "I suspect we probably don't hang out at the same bars."

"I can't remember the last time I hung out at any bar," Pinky said.

"Poor dear," Jake said. "How about the gym?"

Pinky missed her gym in Boca, and so she instantly brightened at the suggestion.

"You can come as my guest, and see if you like it," he said. "It's right on Clematis."

"That would be great," Pinky said.

"There's a step aerobics class I go to. It's practically my religion," Jake said, before glancing over his shoulder to make sure Craig wasn't within earshot. "The guy who teaches it, Kevin? Oh, my God, be still my beating heart."

■

The next morning, Pinky was already in her workout clothes as her two kids sat at the breakfast table in their new school clothes.

"Why can't we still go to school in Boca?" Luna asked.

"Because we live in West Palm Beach," Pinky said. "It's all the same school system. It will be exciting. You'll make new friends."

"Daddy has a new girlfriend," Luna said.

"Oh?" Pinky said, turning from the stove with a spatula in her hand.

"She came to lunch yesterday," Luna said.

Pinky looked at Charlie.

"You're burning the pancakes, Mom."

Pinky turned back to the stove, trying to be casual as she loaded the pancakes on a platter.

"And?" Pinky said. "Is she nice?"

"No," Charlie said, looking away quickly.

Pinky had to do everything in her power not to just put down the platter and hug him right there.

"Her name is Diarrhea," Luna said.

■

A half-hour later, she picked up Jake and drove to the gym.

"I don't usually do step," Pinky said. "So I might get a little behind."

"Honey, I dream about getting a little behind in that class, so please stay out of my slobber zone."

Pinky was surprised at how out of shape she had gotten. About halfway through the class, her legs became leaden, and the choreography became too hard to follow. She quietly slipped out the door and wandered through the gym. She picked up a dumbbell but put it down after only a few curls.

She was never one for weight-lifting and didn't think she could stand the treadmill or the elliptical trainers now, either. She was in a funk.

Cosmo The Lawn King had done it again. Bringing a girlfriend around their children was so wrong. They didn't need to see one of his insignificant others. Unless, maybe, he was already serious with someone. Could it be? He wasn't even divorced yet.

She found the cafe, eager to sit down and take some solace in the form of a chocolate smoothie. She closed her eyes with the first cool pull from the straw.

"Mind if I join you?" she heard.

Standing before her was a tall, handsome man with Prince Valiant-length blond hair and bulging biceps emerging from his ripped T-shirt.

He was already seated across from her by the time she swallowed.

"Travis Plum," he said, extending his big hand.

"Pinky Mulligan," she said, watching her hand being swallowed in his.

They talked for the next 20 minutes. Or, more precisely, he talked for the next 20 minutes. At first, Pinky was in no mood for company, but this Travis guy was a gifted talker, and before long, he had her attention. By the time Jake found her sitting there, she had already handed Travis her business card.

"And here I was feeling sorry for you," Jake said, as they drove home. "I'm there gasping for air while trying to shazzay with Kevin, and you're making time with Sir Lancelot."

"It's not like that," Pinky said. "He's just looking to buy, and I agreed to show him a few places in Pelican Park."

She told Jake as much as she knew. That Travis Plum was a scientist with Scripps Research Institute. He was moving from San Diego to work in the new research lab in Palm Beach County.

"Marital status?" Jake asked.

"Divorced, no kids," Pinky said.

"That's convenient."

"What's that supposed to mean?"

"Nothing," Jake said.

But there was something about Travis Plum that bugged him. Maybe it was the tattoo. Jake couldn't imagine a genetic engineer who would get a dice tattoo on his calf.

"You're just jealous," Pinky said good-naturedly.

"I kid about Kevin the aerobics teacher," Jake said. "But the truth is, Pinky, I'm a one-guy guy. I'd marry Craig tomorrow if it wasn't such a threat to the sanctity of yours and Travis' broken marriages."

"Ouch," Pinky said.

"I'm sorry, darling," Jake said. "I didn't mean to get catty on you."

"That's OK," Pinky said. "I like you anyway."

"That would be a good motto for the neighborhood sign," Jake said. "Pelican Park — We Like You Anyway."

Pinky laughed, but her mind was already elsewhere, thinking about what she would wear when she saw Travis Plum the next day.

■

After dropping Jake back at his house, she returned home, surprised to see her front lawn was freshly mowed. She heard the sound of a mower coming from her back yard. She went inside and looked through the blinds.

The homeless man was out back, cutting careful rows of her lawn. Next to the garage were a dozen little Winn-Dixie bags, each one filled with grass.

"Oh, for crying out loud," Pinky said to herself.

She walked out the back door. He didn't see her at first, not until he turned around and was mowing toward her.

She motioned to him, and he cut the engine. She was glad there was still a good 20 feet between them.

"You don't have to do that," she said, pointing to the little bags full of grass. "I have leaf bags in the garage. They're on the shelf to the right. Use them."

He nodded and waited to see if she had anything else to say before he pulled the cord to start the mower.

"Do you want some water?"

"The hose is fine," he said.

She was about to walk inside, but she stopped.

"Listen, I'm sorry about yesterday. My husband is . . . territorial. I guess that's the most charitable way to describe him."

The homeless man just nodded, his hand still on the pull cord.

She went back in the house, hearing the mower roar to life before she had the back door locked.

Pinky went to her bedroom to look through her clothes. A half-hour after the sound of the mower had stopped, she went to the kitchen to make lunch.

She had thought the homeless man would be long gone, so she was surprised to see him still in her back yard.

She peered through the blinds, watching him as he knelt, pulling weeds, one by one, from her garden. He appeared to be talking to himself.

11

Lunch money

Charlie Hope's first day of eighth grade at Conniston Middle School was uneventful until lunch. He took his tray from the line and surveyed the cafeteria full of strangers.

Most of the other students were already divided into circles of friends that had been hashed out in past years. And these circles were impenetrable to an outsider kid, especially one from Boca who now wished that his mother hadn't insisted he wear the Tommy Hilfiger shirt she'd found at T.J. Maxx.

He settled into an empty seat on the edge of a group of boys, who ignored him. When the boy closest to him got up to get a napkin, he returned to a different seat, leaving Charlie sitting there by himself.

He wondered what The Savages were doing now. They were probably sitting around a table in the Boca Middle cafeteria and working out a song with their new guitar player.

Charlie pretended to read one of his textbooks while he ate, an unimaginable act in his past life. He was nearly done with his meal when he heard the table creak and saw a hand reach across his field of vision and take the brownie from his tray.

Charlie looked up to see a boy in a throwback Washington Bullets basketball jersey calmly eating his brownie while looking at Charlie with casual contempt.

"Whatchu lookin' at, snowflake?"

The boy was big, and he had what appeared to be a self-administered tattoo on his left arm that said "Ray-Ray."

"That's my brownie," Charlie said.

"And now it's mine, little Tommy Hilfiger," Ray-Ray said. "You got a problem with that?"

"That's not right," Charlie said, but he didn't say it as a challenge, or at least he hoped it didn't sound like a challenge.

There was an air of menace about this boy that Charlie could sense right from the start, and he wanted no part of it. So he just put his head down and pretended to read, hoping that trouble would go away, or that one of the cafeteria monitors would swoop in to save him.

But the next thing that happened was the arrival of three more boys.

"Ray-Ray, we was lookin' for you, dawg," one of them said. "Where you be?"

"I'm just here eatin' some dessert with my new homey," Ray-Ray said. "What's your name, boy?"

Charlie ignored him, but two of the boys sat down on either side of him, and Ray-Ray leaned forward close enough so that Charlie could feel his breath on his forehead.

"Are you tryin' to be rude to me?" Ray-Ray said.

Charlie started to stand up, but the boys on either side of him put their arms around his shoulders in what might have looked to a casual observer like a friendly gesture but served only to hold him down.

"Charlie Hope," he said, looking up at Ray-Ray.

"Charlie Dope," Ray-Ray said, which got guffaws from his posse. "I ain't seen you around here before."

Charlie tried to go back to his book, but Ray-Ray said, "I'm talkin' to you, Charlie Dope. Don't be dissing me like this."

Charlie looked up. "I just moved here," he said, his voice a dull monotone, though inside his head it was screaming, "Where is the lunchroom monitor? Where is the lunchroom monitor?"

"From where?"

"Boca."

This drew a big round of laughs from the boys.

"Well, that explains why you look like such a punk," Ray-Ray said. "Boca. I shoulda known."

Charlie looked down again at his book, no longer able to focus on the words.

"I think I'll have some more dessert," Ray-Ray said. "What about you dawgs? Want one of those fine brownies? Our good friend Charlie Dope from Boca is buyin'."

The three other boys all said how much they wanted brownies.

"Ten dollars ought to cover it," Ray-Ray said.

Charlie knew that things had reached the point of no return. If he gave Ray-Ray any money, it was over. The bully wouldn't go away; instead, he'd be back for more and figure out new ways of humiliation.

So Charlie closed his book, took a deep breath and looked up at Ray-Ray.

"I'm not giving you any money," he said.

"That's not a good answer," Ray-Ray said.

His posse hung their heads in mock sadness.

"Leave me alone," Charlie said.

Ray-Ray nodded. And then much to Charlie's surprise, the bully stood up, and, as if on cue, so did the three other boys. So that's how it's done, Charlie thought. Just don't give in to the bullies, and they disappear. His confidence, however, took an immediate U-turn when Ray-Ray said his goodbye before walking away.

"Charlie Dope," Ray-Ray said, "you're more stupid than I thought."

"This neighborhood has such character," Travis Plum was saying.

Pinky had shown Travis both of the houses she represented in Pelican Park, and as they drove block to block, he found more to his liking.

"I wish I could show them to you, but they're Mallow & Mallow listings," Pinky said, "and I don't have the lock combinations yet. But I plan to in the near future."

"Oh, I love the looks of this one," Travis said, pointing to an empty house. "Can we maybe peek in the windows?"

She parked, and they walked around the property, looking in windows and talking about the importance of choosing bold paint colors and making do-it-yourself additions.

"I'm pretty handy," Travis said. "I'd build myself a wooden deck back here, and maybe one of those outdoor kitchens."

Pinky liked talking to Travis Plum, who had what seemed to be encyclopedic knowledge of just about any subject and an ease about him that was enviable.

"When do you start work at Scripps?" she asked.

"Not for a couple of months," he said. "You know, it's just an advance team at this point, and I've still got to go back to California to sell my place in La Jolla."

"Oh, my," Pinky said. "How could anybody leave La Jolla?"

"You've been there?"

"Once. With my husband, before we had kids. We watched the whales breaching off-shore."

"It's a special place," Travis said. "But sometimes, what makes a place special isn't the geography but the people you meet there."

They were looking in a living-room window together, and when he said it, he turned slightly to look at her, and when she looked back at him, he smiled.

"Show me more," he said.

And so they spent the rest of the morning looking at houses in Pelican Park, stopping at the empty ones to walk around the property and size up the potential.

"This is my house," she said, as they drove down her street.

"You live here?" he said.

"For a whole three months now."

"It looks like a great house," Travis said.

"It is. I brought it down to the original wooden floors, and went out and hunted down a whole bunch of Heywood Wakefield furniture."

"I love Heywood Wakefield," he said.

"You know, when I was married, I never bought any because Cosmo — my husband, soon to be ex-husband — never liked it. But now that I'm on my own, I'm making up for lost time."

"I have a few pieces back in San Diego," Travis said.

"Really?"

"I love the simple lines."

"Yes," she said.

"Can I see some of your pieces?"

Pinky pulled in her driveway.

"The place is kind of a mess," she said. "I wasn't expecting to have, you know, company or anything today."

She let him in her house, and he walked from room to room, admiring the furniture and complimenting her on decorating decisions.

"How about an iced tea or something?"

"I've got a better idea," he said. "How about I treat you to lunch?"

"Well, I'm . . . you know, just . . ."

"Unless you've got other plans. I understand."

She hesitated.

"I could pretend it's strictly for business purposes, and that I don't really like you, and am not attracted to you," he said. "If that makes it any easier for you."

The way he said it, and the shy smile he was now giving her, was irresistible. Well, almost.

"You're not planning to take me to Taqueria Guerrero, are you?"

"What's that?"

"Never mind."

"I thought, maybe we'd go to one of those places on Clematis that has sidewalk tables."

"Let's go to that new brasserie, L'Opera," she said.

And they did, having a leisurely lunch over a bottle of wine, with

Pinky gradually relaxing more and more, until she nearly agreed to a second bottle.

The waiter was standing there, and Travis was nodding.

"Don't you think, Pinky?" he said. "Another bottle?"

"Well . . ." she said, nearly adding a "Why not?" until she glanced down at her watch, which was approaching 3 p.m.

"What am I doing?" she said. "The kids will be getting out of school. I have to get home."

"My little Cinderella," Travis said, and then said to the waiter, "Just the check."

When the check arrived, Travis dug into his pants pocket and frowned. He held a money clip with a small number of bills in it.

"My credit card," he said. "I must have left it on the dresser. I feel like such a fool. I don't have enough cash on me."

"Oh," Pinky said. "I have plastic."

"This is awful," he said, sliding the bill over to her. "We'll split it. I insist."

"OK," she said.

It was nearly $100 before the tip, and Travis handed her a $10 bill folded over five singles, saying, "I'll give you the rest the next time I see you."

Pinky put the money in her wallet, barely looking at it — her mood was still high though her mind was gradually shifting to her motherly responsibilities.

She took him to his car, a sleek, new black BMW, and then she drove home. She was walking to her front door when she heard a toot and turned to see Travis idling his car in front of her house.

"Pinky, I've got something for you," he yelled out.

She walked around to the driver's side of his car, half expecting him to give her some more money. But instead, he said, "I think you were in too much of a hurry to give me a proper kiss before, and I need one."

"You do?" she asked, amused by the mock seriousness of his tone.

"Yes, right now," he said, and as she started to lean toward the window, he guided the back of her head toward him, kissing her there as she stood next to the car, leaving half her body draped over the door.

She straightened up, and without a word, he drove away, leaving her there in the street, her lipstick smeared, her hair mussed, and her teenage son standing a few yards away, his backpack over one shoulder and a look of revulsion on his face.

"Oh, hello, Charlie," she said. "That was Travis, a new . . . client.

We were just talking about a house. How was school? Did you . . . Charlie!"

Her son's lip was bloody, his shirt torn.

"My God! What happened?"

"Nothing."

He was already walking past her and into the house.

12

Bad connection

Charlie Hope came up with a story, telling his mother he had bloodied his lip and ripped his shirt playing touch football during lunch hour.

The next morning, he asked if it would be all right to bring his lunch instead of buying in the cafeteria.

"The food's that bad?" his mother asked.

"It was yesterday," Charlie said.

"All I can make you is peanut butter and jelly," his mother said. "I would have bought cold cuts if I'd known."

"Peanut butter and jelly is fine," he said.

"It is?"

"And can you pick me up after school?"

"I thought you were looking forward to walking home this year."

"It's kinda hot."

Charlie's plan was to avoid Ray-Ray and that maybe if he and the bully didn't cross paths, Ray-Ray would find somebody else to pick on. So, Charlie would try to eat his lunch in his fourth-period science room, rather than the cafeteria. And he'd stay in the safety of the parent pickup line after school until his mother drove up to take him home.

He didn't want to underestimate Ray-Ray as he had done the previous day, when the thug and his posse were waiting for Charlie on the way home from school.

"That wasn't right, you disrespectin' me at lunch," Ray-Ray had told Charlie as he fell in step.

Charlie had thought about running, but it was pointless. Two of Ray-Ray's boys were behind him, with another up ahead.

"Leave me alone," Charlie had said, keeping his eyes straight ahead, so his face wouldn't betray his fear.

"I don't believe I heard that," Ray-Ray said.

"Then clean your ears," Charlie said.

The next moment, he was down, jumped from behind. His lip grazed the sidewalk, and as one of the boys kneeled on his back. Ray-Ray pulled Charlie's wallet out of his pants pocket, removing all the money he had — three dollar bills. He tossed the empty wallet down by Charlie's face.

"This ain't enough, Charlie Dope," Ray-Ray said. "Tomorrow, you best bring more money to school."

At first, Charlie thought he'd blurt it all to his mother and that maybe she'd go to school and tell the principal. But somehow, he had the sense that if he got Ray-Ray in trouble, it might spare him in the short run but would only unleash some greater payback in the future.

Then Charlie thought that maybe he ought to just ask his mother for $20, making up some bogus story about a school activity fee or something. But he also had a sense that if he gave Ray-Ray any money, he'd be marked for the rest of the year as Ray-Ray's human ATM machine.

So he opted for just staying out of Ray-Ray's way.

His plan worked smoothly through the school day, with Charlie always blending with the crowd during class changes. During lunch, the science teacher was more than happy to have a student who wanted to help him inventory his materials in the lab. And after the last bell of the day, Charlie spent as little time as possible lingering by his locker. He raced to the parent pickup area, happy to see an assistant principal there using a bullhorn to announce arriving parents.

Charlie put down his backpack, and for the first time that day, he relaxed, leaning against the wall and waiting for his mother's cream-colored Lexus to join the long line of cars.

Then the cellphone in his backpack rang. He fished it out, and the first inkling of dread hit him when the caller ID screen displayed who it was.

■

Pinky had spent the day walking the neighborhood, going door-to-door to introduce herself as both a new neighbor and a new real-estate agent. Despite herself, she kept coming up with another reason to go home for something — knowing full well that the only reason was to check her answering machine to see if Travis Plum had called. He hadn't.

The only call was from Luna's new fifth-grade teacher, a Mrs. Swenson, who had a gravelly smoker's voice and a rapid-fire delivery.

"Mrs. Hope," the teacher said, "call me at your convenience. It's about your daughter."

Like any mother, Pinky assumed the worst, already visualizing her daughter bleeding from some ghastly playground injury. She dialed the school right away and was relieved to find out that her daughter was fine.

"Your daughter wrote something in school today that I think you should see," Mrs. Swenson said.

"Well, of course," Pinky said. "I'll look for it in her backpack."

"It's not a take-home assignment," the teacher said.

"Oh."

"It's best you come in. We should probably talk about it."

So Pinky drove to Belvedere Elementary that afternoon, arranging to meet Mrs. Swenson at the end of the school day.

"Anna Swenson," the teacher said, holding out her hand but not offering a smile. "Luna's in the media center."

"Does she know I'm here?"

"No," the teacher said, leading Pinky into her classroom.

Pinky sat down at one of the desks, while Mrs. Swenson leafed through a pile of papers. She spoke to Pinky without looking at her.

"I've been teaching for 40 years," she said. "I've got four kids of my own and three grandkids."

She found the paper she had been looking for.

"I know a cry for help when I see one," she said, handing the paper to Pinky.

Pinky recognized her daughter's loopy cursive handwriting.

"I ask the kids every year to write about their summer as a timed writing exercise," the teacher said. "Most kids write only a few lines, describing some trip to The Rapids water park or their summer camp."

Pinky had begun reading, and as she did, she felt the color rising in her cheeks.

"I know if I were Luna's mom, I'd want her teacher to show me this," Mrs. Swenson said.

But Pinky had stopped listening, riveted to the paper, which began with a heartbreaking line that made her gasp: "I had the worst summer of my life. I don't live in a home anymore. I just live in a house."

Her daughter wrote about everything. Her father's new girlfriend. Her mother's fascination with new furniture. Being shipped off to her cousins against her will. All her old friends being gone. Her parents arguing every time they saw each other. Her mother using a new last name as if she weren't even her mother anymore.

"Sometimes I wish I was never alive," Luna wrote. "Or that this is all just a bad dream and I'm going to wake up and find out nothing was real."

Pinky had to stop reading. Mrs. Swenson tossed her a box of tissues.

"My poor little girl," Pinky said.

"Kids see everything," the teacher said. "And feel everything."

"What'll I do?"

The teacher shrugged.

"That's not for me to say," she said. "Just keep in mind: Adults can get divorced, but kids don't have that luxury."

"Her brother seems to be taking everything in stride."

Then Pinky remembered. She was supposed to be picking Charlie up at school.

"Oh, no," she said, digging into her purse for the cellphone. "Excuse me, I need to call my son."

He picked up on the fourth ring.

"Mom?"

"Hi, Charlie."

"Why aren't you here?" he said. "I'm waiting at parent pickup."

"Charlie, something came up, and I can't get there anytime soon."

"Something came up?"

"Yes."

"Like what?"

"Just . . . something, Charlie. I need you to walk home today."

"Something like that guy? The guy you were kissing yesterday in the street? You're gross, Mom!"

And then he hung up. Pinky was stunned. Her son had never hung up on her before.

"Charlie? Charlie?"

She looked over at Mrs. Swenson and wished the teacher wasn't sitting there, hands folded, looking back at her.

"Bad connection," Pinky said.

"Uh-huh."

Charlie began walking home, his fear now mixed with a liberal dose of anger. Nothing happened at first. Charlie began to think that maybe he'd be home free. But when he reached Belvedere Road, he heard the familiar voice.

"Hey, it's Charlie Dope," Ray-Ray said, falling in beside him with his posse. "I thought you was maybe out sick today."

Charlie kept walking, ignoring the boys.

"Me and the fellas been feelin' a little thirsty, and we hear you're buying today," Ray-Ray said.

"You heard wrong," Charlie said.

The boys spun him around, discovering Charlie didn't have a wallet. They yanked the backpack off his shoulders, unzipped it and emptied it on the sidewalk, sending a shower of paper all over the street.

"Where's your money, punk?" Ray-Ray said.

"I haven't got any," Charlie said, bending to snag some of the papers before they flew away.

Ray-Ray grabbed him by the shirt collar and stood him back up.

"I'm afraid that's going to cost you."

Charlie summoned up all his courage and shoved the bigger boy, causing him to stagger back a few steps.

Ray-Ray smiled.

"Oh, you bein' the fool now, boy."

Charlie waited for the fists to start flying. But someone, a boy, stepped between him and Ray-Ray. All Charlie saw was his back, and

then he heard the boy's deep baritone voice.

"That's enough, Ray-Ray."

"Terrell, we ain't got no beef with you."

"I'm giving you and your boys five seconds to get outta here, or I'm going to start whuppin' your behinds."

"Terrell, you don't have to be that way. This boy owes us some money, and we just collecting the debt."

"Five . . . four . . . three . . ."

"OK, OK, Terrell. We gone."

And they were. All four of them. The big boy turned to face Charlie, who was awestruck with gratitude.

"Thanks. I'm Charlie Hope."

"I know who you are," the boy said. "Your mom's that new real-estate lady. My dad's Bishop Crumley, the pastor at The Holy Blood of the Everlasting Redeemer. And this is my sister, Bea."

Charlie hadn't noticed anybody else. He turned around to see a pretty black girl bending down to pick up his books and corral some of the loose papers as they danced down the sidewalk.

"You best walk to school with us for a while until Ray-Ray gets the idea not to mess with you anymore."

Charlie was still looking at this big eighth-grader's 13-year-old sister and blushing deeply as she looked back at him and smiled.

"That'd be great," Charlie said.

13

Algebra and chocolate

Mark Stone sat on his milk crate behind the abandoned gas station on Belvedere. He saw it all unfold. The way Ray-Ray and his crew quickly swooped down on their prey, encircling the boy they called Charlie Dope.

He'd seen this boy before. His mother owned the house in Pelican Park, the one with the lawn that Stone cut.

"Don't fight them," Stone said under his breath as he watched from afar, hoping this boy wouldn't make a mistake.

But the boy did try to fight back, and in that moment, Stone felt both admiration and pity for him.

"No," Stone mouthed, for he knew what Ray-Ray was capable of doing.

Stone sat watching with a kind of dread, sensing what was to come. But then he saw the arrival of the big kid and his sister, and how it changed the fate of Charlie, driving Ray-Ray and his crew away. A miracle, really.

What if the boy's rescuers hadn't come? Would Stone eventually have run across the street to try to save the boy? He couldn't answer his own question. Maybe his own fear would have taken root, planting him right there on that milk crate and preventing him from doing anything but watching and saying "No" under his breath.

Stone wondered whether he had the physical bravery to do something like that, and a good part of him doubted it. And for that, he felt doubly shamed.

But his shame was quickly replaced by fascination as he watched the saved boy fall into step with his two saviors, and he saw the way the girl and Charlie exchanged glances. He watched the three of them walk away, out of sight, unaware that some of the papers from Charlie's backpack were still fluttering down the street.

Stone got off his milk crate and walked along Belvedere, picking up each piece of paper from the boy's backpack until he could find no more. He looked at what he found. Most were handouts from teachers, outlining class rules, and schedules of assignments. There were also notices to parents, invitations to join the PTA and to volunteer in the office.

But what interested Stone the most was an algebra assignment, a single sheet of paper with six problems on it. The words "Due tomorrow" were written in pencil on the top margin of the page, and there was a name, too: Charlie Hope.

A good name, Stone thought. Not a dope, but a Hope.

Charlie and the others were nowhere to be seen. The boy, Stone figured, was probably already close to his home in Pelican Park.

The homeless man walked back to his milk crate and looked at the algebra paper again. He hadn't seen algebra in years. He scratched his head as he considered each problem, seeing if he still remembered how to solve for X.

He stashed the rest of the papers inside the abandoned gas station, among his other things, and took the algebra paper with him, beginning his walk. It would take him just about half an hour to get to the West Palm Beach Public Library.

He wondered whether somebody there would lend him a pencil.

After taking her daughter home from school, Pinky called her husband on his cellphone, willing herself to be civil, yet direct.

"Cosmo, I'm worried about the kids. We can get divorced, but they don't have that luxury," she said, surprised to hear herself uttering the words of Luna's teacher.

Cosmo, true to form, took things the wrong way.

"So, you're missing me," he said.

"This is about the kids, not us."

"That boyfriend, the frizzy-haired lawyer without the TV, he didn't work out?"

"Cosmo, can you please just put your enormous ego on the shelf for a moment and listen?"

"Or maybe that homeless guy who does your lawn, he doing a crappy job?"

"Are you finished?"

She explained that their daughter was unhappy and their son was little more than a closed book, unwilling to share more than name, rank and serial number in answer to most of her questions.

"That's just because he's a boy," Cosmo said. "There's nothing wrong with Charlie."

"How do you know?" she asked. "You don't even live with him."

"That wasn't my choice."

"And what am I supposed to do, just put up with your . . . your philandering?" she said, the emotion rising in her voice. "By the way, nice move introducing your new mattress to them already. That was smooth."

"Deirdre understands me."

"Diarrhea."

"What?"

This had become just the kind of conversation she was trying to avoid. They were talking about each other when Pinky had wanted to talk about the kids. They had begun finding ways to hurt each other, when her aim was to see whether there was some way to comfort their children.

"Listen, Cosmo. I didn't call you to fight."

"Had me fooled."

They were both quiet for a moment, and Pinky could hear the road noise from I-95 coming through her husband's cellphone and the panting of Gomez in the background. She took a deep breath.

"Can you come up here tonight? Let's have dinner as a family. The kids started school, and I think it would be nice and reassuring if we gave them an evening of our undivided attention."

"Wow, that's really nice of you, allowing me to see my own children."

"You don't get it, do you?"

"You running out of my money, is that it?"

She willed herself not to get detoured.

"It's allowing them to see us together, Cosmo. That's what's important. We're going to have to figure out how to act civil with each other in front of them. Before it's too late."

"You been watchin' Dr. Phil?"

"I've been at a conference with Luna's teacher," she said. "Our daughter is very unhappy."

There were tremors in her last few words.

"So what do I gotta do?" he finally asked.

"Be here at 6," she said, "and bring Gomez."

There was a clicking on her phone line.

"Can you just hold a second, Cosmo? Another call is coming in."

Pinky switched lines, and said, "Hello?"

"Hi, Pinky."

"Travis."

She had wanted him to call all day, and now that he had called, she didn't want to talk to him. It must have come through in her voice.

"Did I call at a bad time?"

"No. Yes," she said. "Actually, I'm on the other line, and it's important."

"OK, I won't keep you then. I just . . . well, I just went to the gym again today, and I . . . I missed seeing you there. That's all."

"Oh," she said. "I missed you, too."

"You were at the gym?"

"No, I just . . . Travis, will you be at the gym tomorrow?"

"Just give me a time."

"Nine?"

"See you then," he said, and then she clicked back to the other line.

"Your boyfriend?" Cosmo said.

"Please, Cosmo. Let's get back to talking about the kids."

"Who was that on the phone?" he asked.

"I'm joining a gym here," she said. "It was just about that."

"But you already have a gym membership."

"In Boca. Where I don't live anymore."

"That wasn't my choice," he said.

"Haven't we already covered this topic?"

■

That night, they appeared to be a harmonious, nuclear family out for dinner. They were eating at The Cheesecake Factory in City-Place, sitting in one of the booths, the boy next to his father, the girl next to her mother.

"And so Gomez went running after the rabbit, and this old lady comes flyin' out of the house — I mean just haulin' booty — and she's yelling, 'Mister, please save my Fluffy from that monster!' "

Luna went into a fit of convulsive laughter, nearly gagging on her chicken fingers. She, of all of them, loved the Gomez stories her father told. Pinky was certain that most of them were complete fiction, but like her kids, she found herself easily enthralled by the way Cosmo Hope could light up a room.

Some people are just born with it, and Cosmo was one of those people. It's how she had fallen in love with him in the first place. And it's undoubtedly how a string of women after her would fall in love with him, too.

"And so I say, 'That noble dog is not a monster, madam, he's just an Attack Chihuahua.' "

Even Charlie was laughing now. And Pinky's mind went back to the first story her husband ever told her. She was at a fraternity party at Florida State, and this cute boy she didn't know handed her a fresh beer and said, "Did you know that there's a secret sect of Catholic monks who live underneath Doak Campbell Stadium?"

"Excuse me?" Pinky had said, taking the beer but keeping her eyes on his hundred-watt smile.

"That's why the football team's playbook is done in calligraphy," he had said, sitting next to her and making himself comfortable for the next 20 years.

She looked at him now, missing the end of his Gomez story but catching him looking back at her as their children laughed. She could see in his expression something like triumph and satisfaction, something that told her that he knew, even if she didn't, that he'd always have a piece of her. And of them.

"Who's ready for dessert?" he announced.

"Count me out," she said. "I'm absolutely stuffed."

The kids, of course, were already looking over the dessert menu. While they did, Pinky excused herself to go to the restroom. On her way, she looked across the crowded restaurant, and much to her surprise, she spotted the unmistakable blond mane of Travis Plum. He had his back to her and was walking to a table on the other side of the room.

"Travis," Pinky called out, but he didn't hear her.

She was out of sight from her family, so she started to follow Travis, who had turned a corner to another section of the restaurant. She was about 10 paces behind him, and ready to call out his name again when she saw the table for two that was his destination.

A pretty, younger woman in a black cocktail dress greeted him and smiled. Pinky did a U-turn and headed back to the restrooms, the color rising in her cheeks.

By the time she returned to the table, dessert had already arrived.

"You OK, Mom?" Luna said, the only one to sense something different about her.

"Yes. Fine."

"You look sick," Luna said.

"No, something just didn't agree with me," she said.

Cosmo had an enormous brownie on his plate with a scoop of chocolate ice cream on top of it.

He slid a spoon across the table to her — his spoon, which was already coated with chocolate ice cream. She waved him off, but Cosmo just smiled. He knew better.

"Take your crack, sweetheart."

Despite herself, she picked up his spoon and dug in for an enormous bite, closing her eyes as the chocolate performed its dependable magic.

14

Sister, sister

At first, Mark Stone wasn't sure how he could get the completed algebra assignment back to Charlie. It was out of the question to just knock on the door of the boy's house. Too many things could go wrong with that, and besides, Stone thought it best to remain anonymous.

His next idea was to leave the paper somewhere along Charlie's walking path to school. But that wasn't a reliable method of return.

It wasn't until Stone had leafed through some of the other papers that he saw the best way. One of the boy's papers Stone had found was an information sheet from another class. On it, Charlie Hope had written his e-mail address.

So after Stone finished the algebra assignment at the West Palm Beach Public Library, he used one of the computers there to write the boy the following e-mail:

I found your algebra assignment and some other papers on the street. I'm leaving them for you in a manila envelope at the pay phone on the southeast corner of Lake Avenue and Belvedere Road.

■

Stone was watching from a distance the next morning as Charlie Hope walked to school with Terrell and Bea Crumley. He saw the three of them cross Belvedere and head straight for the pay phone.

■

Jake Fisher drove Pinky to the gym that morning. She nearly told him she had changed her mind and reconsidered joining.

Discovering Travis Plum in the restaurant with another woman the previous night had been a shock. She had thought there was a real spark between the two of them, and he had seemed to be equally infatuated with her.

But maybe this is what the dating scene was like when you got to be in your 40s. So many people out there were damaged goods in some way — herself included.

"I've got an idea for you to break the Mallow & Mallow stranglehold on Pelican Park," Jake said. "Are you listening?"

"Sure," Pinky said, turning toward him and braving a smile.

Jake's idea was to make Pinky Mulligan the gay-friendly real-estate agent.

"Marvin Mallow is a homophobe," Jake said. "It practically seeps out of his pores. He has never advertised in gay publications, and he has made some remarks about his goal of making Pelican Park a 'family-friendly community.' Hint, hint. The reason Pelican Park isn't as gay as it could be is because of Marvin Mallow's policy of homo cleansing."

"You really think he's that bad?" Pinky asked.

"Ask Craig," Jake said. "Craig's not as militant as I am, but even Craig agrees about Mallow. It was Craig's idea to name our cat Leviticus. Just to get under Marvin's skin at homeowners association meetings."

"Leviticus?"

"My dear," Jake said, "you are tragically uninformed about holy gay bashing. It's the section of the Bible that sanctimonious bigots use to justify their flat-earth mentality."

Pinky had managed to live 42 years without giving much thought to sexual politics. She had never looked at herself as either gay-friendly or gay-hostile.

"Why do you assume I'm different from Marvin Mallow?" she asked Jake.

He looked at her now, and said, "Do you want to be my friend?"

"Yes," she said.

"And you introduced me to your children," he said. "You're gay-friendly, Pinky Mulligan. You may not know it yet. But I do."

"Well, I'm glad you're so good at figuring people out," she said. "Because I'm sure not."

Then she told him about seeing Travis in the restaurant and wishing she could just turn around and go home.

"It's a jungle out there, honey," Jake said, patting her on the knee.

"What do I say to him?"

"Just be yourself," Jake said.

"And how about if I don't know who I am?"

Pinky walked into the gym, relieved to find that Travis wasn't there. She began jogging on a treadmill. Five minutes later, she saw him walk in. She pretended she didn't see him and was thankful for her headphones.

He stepped onto the next treadmill and lightly touched her shoulder. She turned and coolly nodded to him. She could see his lips moving, but she didn't bother taking off her headphones.

She jogged for another five minutes, then got off the treadmill and walked away. She reached the water fountain, but before she could take a drink, she felt a tap on her shoulder.

"Hello, Travis," she said. She bent over, and took a long drink.

"How are you?" Travis asked, when she was done.

She shrugged.

"Something wrong?" he asked.

"So, who's your girlfriend?"

"Pinky, I don't understand."

She tried to keep her voice calm but wasn't being very successful.

"Don't lie to me," she said and walked away.

He followed her.

"Pinky, I was looking so forward to seeing you today. I'm confused here. Help me out."

She glared at him.

"Maybe you're confusing me with the woman in the little black dress at The Cheesecake Factory last night."

She watched as his expression changed from surprise to something else — she wasn't sure what — and finally to a big smile followed by laughter.

"What's so funny?" she said.

"You're jealous of my sister."

"Your sister?"

"She's a third-year law school student at Stetson. She's in South Florida for a few days doing some job interviews. I took her to dinner last night. Oh, I wish you had come up and introduced yourself."

Pinky was starting to feel foolish.

"She even asked if I had found anybody special," Travis said, "and I told her about meeting you and that although we had only met, I felt kind of special with you."

"Oh," Pinky said. "I just thought . . ."

"You would have loved meeting her, too," Travis said.

Pinky put her head in her hands.

"I feel so dippy."

He put a hand on her shoulder.

"I know how you can make it up to me," he said. "You can buy me dinner tonight."

On the way home from the gym, Jake wanted all the details.

"From the looks of that goodbye kiss, I'd say you and Travis are back on again."

Pinky told him everything, and Jake listened quietly. When she was through talking, he seemed to be ready to say something. Then he stopped.

"What?" Pinky said.

"Nothing," Jake said. "I'm happy for you."

"You were going to say something," she said.

Jake hesitated before talking.

"He's not a natural blond."

Charlie Hope couldn't believe his good fortune. Now that he was under the protective custody of Terrell Crumley, Ray-Ray and his thugs gave him a wide berth. Terrell was the center on the school's basketball team, which made him part of a crowd that even a guy like Ray-Ray had to respect. To take on Terrell Crumley was to take on a dozen of the toughest boys in school.

Plus, Ray-Ray had made the mistake last year of trying to make a play for Bea, Terrell's little sister. Bea wanted no part of it, and when she complained to her big brother, Terrell had a brief but legendary fight with Ray-Ray and three members of his posse outside school one day.

Ray-Ray knew that the next time he fought with Terrell, he'd have to pull his knife on the bigger boy, and Ray-Ray wasn't ready just yet to deal with the consequences of stabbing the star of what could be the district champion team. So, as long as Charlie Dope was with Terrell, the skinny little white boy from Boca was hands-off.

"What church you belong to?" Terrell asked Charlie as they walked home from school that afternoon.

"We don't go to church," Charlie said.

Terrell just nodded, but Bea immediately said, "You ought to come to our church. "

Terrell looked at her as if she were crazy.

"There are no white boys at The Holy Blood of the Everlasting Redeemer," he told his sister.

"Do you sing?" Bea asked Charlie. "I'm in the choir."

Charlie gulped. He could only look at Bea for a second or two, then he would have to turn away because he'd find himself staring at her perfect coffee-brown skin and full lips, and it would make him feel weird.

White boys, he thought, weren't supposed to like black girls.

"I sing," Charlie said. "I used to play guitar in a rock band, and I sang background."

"We need a guitar in the church band. Don't we, Terrell?" Bea said.

"You're unbelievable," Terrell told her.

"What kind of music do you play?" Bea asked Charlie.

"Grunge."

"That will be great," she said.

"No, it won't!" Terrell said.

"We'll make it work," Bea said, putting a hand on Charlie's arm, which nearly made him jump. "If you want it to work, we can make it work."

He looked at her now and forced himself to hold her gaze.

"I . . . yeah, it's worth a try," he said.

Then he put his head down and walked in silence.

"Wait till the bishop finds out about this," Terrell said.

"Terrell Crumley, don't you go poisoning Dad with your non-sense."

"Little Jezebel."

"Big Bird."

Nobody said anything for a while. Terrell finally spoke.

"Charlie Hope, I shoulda let those boys just beat you up."

Charlie looked up, relieved to see the big boy smiling down at him.

"Don't listen to him," Bea said. "Can you make rehearsal Wednesday night?"

■

Mark Stone sat on his milk crate, watching the parade of school kids crossing Belvedere on their way home. He was happy to see Charlie Hope with that huge black boy again. And Stone was even happier to see Charlie pause by the phone booth at the corner of Lake Avenue, reach into his backpack and pull out a manila envelope. The boy put the envelope in the same spot that Stone had used that morning.

After waiting more time than necessary, Stone emerged from his spot behind the abandoned gas station and crossed the street. He took the envelope from the phone booth and kept walking, not opening it until he had circled the block and returned to his milk crate.

There was a photocopy of another assignment in there, an essay due in a week. And there was a note, too, written in Charlie's pinched cursive style.

"Thanks for the algebra," it said. "Do you do English?"

Stone tucked the paper in his pocket and headed for the library.

15
Night visitors

That night, while his mother was out with Travis Plum, Charlie Hope received another e-mail:

Charlie:

I helped you on the algebra because it was an emergency, and I didn't want you to start off on the wrong foot at school. But it was never my intention to do your homework for you.

However, I'd be happy to tutor you in your studies. Actually, I'd be thrilled. But you need to do the work yourself, and use me only as an extra resource.

As for further communications, please continue to use the phone booth. This is a public computer, so responding to this e-mail isn't possible.

— Anon

Weird name, Charlie thought.

He was both disappointed and pleased about the e-mail: disappointed that he hadn't found somebody who would do his work for him but happy to have this secret friend who was willing to help him.

He took out a sheet of paper and wrote the response he would leave in the phone booth the following morning.

Anon:

OK. That's cool.

He was interrupted by a car's headlights that briefly flashed in his window. When he looked out a minute later, he saw his mom and that guy, Travis, sitting in his car in the driveway. The lights of the car were off, and they were necking.

"Gross me out," Charlie said to himself.

He picked up his guitar and strummed a few chords, and within seconds, he imagined himself wailing a solo to *Purple Haze* in front of Bea and the rest of the congregation at The Holy Blood of the Everlasting Redeemer.

His mother still hadn't come inside, but Charlie didn't want to look out the window again. He put down his guitar pick, grabbed his pencil and continued his note to Anon.

I got this girl I like. Her name is Bea.

He was still writing 10 minutes later when he heard his mother unlock the front door.

◼

The following night, Pinky Mulligan woke up with a sound coming from her bathroom. It was nearly 2 in the morning, according to the lighted dial of her bedside clock. While her eyes focused on the clock, her ears were trying to make sense of the sloshing sound coming from the adjoining bathroom.

Then it dawned on her what it must be.

"Luna, that you? Oh, poor baby."

Pinky got out of bed and ran in the dark to the bathroom door. Charlie used the bathroom on the other side of the house. The splashing sound, Pinky concluded, must have been her daughter throwing up in the toilet bowl with the onset of a stomach virus.

Pinky turned on the bathroom light, expecting to see her daughter bent over the bowl. But what she actually saw made her scream.

A drenched rat was trying to make its way out of her toilet bowl, struggling to get its paws up over the ledge.

"Eeeeee! Eeeeee! Eeeeee!" Pinky screamed as she stood there, paralyzed by the sight. The terror in her voice must have given the rat the extra adrenaline it needed to finally scale the bowl and flop on top of the ledge. A second later, it tumbled onto the tile floor, and with nowhere to hide in the bathroom, it made a dash between Pinky's legs, running for the relative safety of her bedroom.

"Eeeeee!" Pinky screamed again, nearly fainting at the sight of the rat scurrying underneath her and into her sanctum. She turned and ran out of the bathroom and out of the bedroom, closing the door behind her to trap the rat inside there.

The thought of the toilet-soaked rat getting acquainted with her bedroom completely unnerved her. And her screaming had awakened both her kids, who now stood beside her in the living room.

"Can we keep it?" Luna asked.

"It's a filthy rat!" Pinky said. "A hairy, disgusting, disease-carrying rat."

"I don't care," Luna said.

"I'll get it for you, Mom," Charlie said, going for the kitchen broom.

He disappeared behind the bedroom door with the broom. Pinky listened on the other side of the door for sounds of combat. But she heard nothing.

She cracked the door, peeking inside to see her son standing on her bed with the broom. He looked as frightened as she was.

"I don't see it," Charlie said. "Are you sure it wasn't just a dream, Mom?"

"Come on out here," she said.

He gladly complied, closing the door quickly as he left the room.

"Maybe it was just your imagination," the boy was saying, but she was already walking to the kitchen and thinking about whom she could call.

Maybe the pest-control companies had a 24-hour service, she thought. She tried three numbers, getting recordings each time.

"Let's call Daddy," Luna said.

"No," Pinky said.

She didn't want to bring her husband here for this. It would be just the sort of thing that Cosmo would gloat over, and he'd probably end up holding the dead rat in her face and chasing her around the house with it for the amusement of the kids at her expense.

"I know who we can call," Pinky said. "My friend, Travis."

Her budding romance with Travis hadn't reached the stage where she felt comfortable introducing him to her children, but this was different. He'd be coming over to help her with an emergency. It wasn't as if this were some sort of date.

"Who's Travis?" Luna said.

"Mom's new boyfriend," Charlie said.

"He's just a friend," Pinky said.

"Yeah, right," Charlie said.

"Mom's got a boyfriend?" Luna said.

"Duh!" Charlie said to her sister. "Didn't you see the guy who picked her up for dinner last night?"

"The one that looks like a prince?" Luna said.

"More like a princess," Charlie said.

"Children!" Pinky said. "That's quite enough."

She walked out of the room as she dialed the phone number to Travis' apartment. She was already thinking about how she would have to use her son's bathroom to wash her face and get her hair presentable.

But instead of hearing his groggy, sleepy voice, the phone rang six unanswered times, and then his chirpy phone-message recording began.

"Travis, this is Pinky," she said, after waiting for the beep. "Sorry to call so late, but I guess you're not home, anyway. I just have . . . a kind of emergency here. If you get this message anytime soon, please call."

She hung up, wondering why he wasn't home at 2 in the morning when he was planning to meet her at the gym at 9.

She dialed Sindee next.

"I'm so sorry to wake you, Sin."

"That's OK, I was just working."

"At this hour?"

"This is one of my peak Internet traffic times. Guys like to watch me sleep. In fact, right now, there are probably dozens of guys sitting in front of their computers looking at me talking on the phone and trying to imagine what I'm saying and who I'm talking to."

"A rat climbed out of my toilet bowl and ran into my bedroom," Pinky said.

"Keep talking," Sindee said, "and disregard any moaning sounds I make while I pretend to be totally turned on by this conversation."

"The rat's in my bedroom someplace," Pinky said.

"Unhhh."

"I closed the door."

"Yes . . . mmm."

"But I'm not going in there until that rat's been killed."

"Oh, oh, oh . . ."

"Sindee!"

"Keep talking, I'm listening."

"Never mind," Pinky said. "You go back to work, or to sleep, or whatever it is you're doing. I'm sorry to bother you."

Pinky heard Sindee's voice say, "Don't . . . stop!" but it was too late for Pinky to determine whether the words were an effort to keep her from hanging up or just some more play-acting for her subscribers.

Pinky hung up the phone. Both kids sat there staring at her. Luna was the first one to speak.

"I'm calling Daddy," she said, and when she picked up the phone, Pinky didn't try to stop her.

Pinky put on a kettle for tea, and the three of them waited in the kitchen for the next half-hour, until they heard a knock on the door. Pinky opened it, expecting to see her husband. Instead, it was her neighbor, Santiago Klein, the public defender.

"Sindee called me," he said. "She said you had a household emergency."

Pinky hadn't seen Santiago since they'd had dinner together, an evening that ended awkwardly for her.

"Oh, Santiago," she said. "Come in."

"How's Mark working out?" he asked.

"Who's Mark?"

"Mark Stone. The man who's doing your lawn."

"Oh," she said. "Fine."

Then she heard her husband's truck pull up in front of the house.

A moment later, before she had time to fully explain to Santiago what was going on, Cosmo The Lawn King walked through the door with Gomez, much to the delight of the kids.

"Get the rat, Gomez!" Cosmo said, putting the dog on the floor.

The gap-toothed Chihuahua went straight to Santiago Klein and bit him on the ankle.

"Evenin', Pinky," Cosmo said to his wife, while the young lawyer danced around the floor, trying to shake the Chihuahua off his leg.

"Smart dog," Cosmo said, winking at his kids.

Pinky spent the next 10 minutes getting ice for Santiago and ministering to his wound, which, due to the general lack of teeth in Gomez's mouth, hadn't been one that drew blood.

"Ah, it's nothing," Cosmo said, who gave a cursory glance at the lawyer's leg before taking the broom from his son and walking into the bedroom with Gomez and closing the door behind him.

"I'm so sorry, Santiago," Pinky said. "I didn't know Sindee was going to call you."

She heard Gomez barking, furniture being moved and the sound of broom hitting the tile.

"I hope he's not killing the creature," Santiago said.

That's when Pinky remembered that one of the stickers on the back of Santiago's car was for PETA — People For the Ethical Treatment of Animals.

"There are ways to trap the rat and release it to the outside world," he said.

The sound grew more furious in the bedroom. More furniture was being moved. More whapping of the broom.

"I think things are under control," Pinky said, helping Santiago up. "Thanks so much for coming to help."

"We could have baited it with a Have-a-Heart trap and a little cheese," Santiago said. "It probably got into your house by accident. It would be cruel to kill an animal under these circumstances."

Pinky was rooting for the rat's death. But she thought it would be polite not to argue with Klein and beneficial to get him out of the house before her alpha-male husband completed his mission in the other room.

She was almost successful. She had her hand on the doorknob, and the protesting PETA lifetime member halfway out of her house, when her triumphant husband exploded out of the bedroom, holding the bludgeoned rat by the tail and announcing his victory.

"Got the nasty rascal!"

16

Ghosts that tap and sigh

The next day, Mark Stone watched as Charlie Hope left another message in the phone booth.

Stone had been afraid his e-mail to the boy would be the last communication between them. So he was relieved to see Charlie drop off another envelope on his way to school, and it was even better to read it — a chatty, friendly missive to an anonymous friend.

Stone was reading it from his milk-crate perch when Santiago Klein pulled up, parked and limped over. Stone stared quizzically at Klein's bandaged ankle.

"I was mauled by a toothless Chihuahua," Klein told him.

"You look like hell," Stone said.

"So do you," Klein said.

"Yeah, but I'm homeless."

"Good point," Klein said. "I didn't get a good night's sleep," he explained.

He reached into his pocket and handed Stone two $20 bills. "It's for mowing that woman's lawn," Klein said. "She paid me."

"Pinky Mulligan," Stone said, making no motion to take the bills.

"Take the money, Mark."

"What for?"

"Because it's legal tender. Because you don't have any. Because everything in this world costs money."

"Not everything," Stone said. "When did you become such a capitalist, Santiago?"

"Don't insult me," the lawyer said. "Take the money. I think if you try hard, you can find some way to put it to use."

"I probably could," Stone said, thinking about the boy's note in his hand.

"Good," Klein said, sticking the bills in Stone's shirt pocket. "By the way, the lawn needs to be mowed again, and I have some more clothes for you out by my shower."

Stone smiled at the lawyer, his truest friend in the world.

"Thanks, Santiago," he said. "I didn't mean that bit about you turning into a capitalist."

Two hours later, Stone walked into the the Barnes & Noble bookstore at CityPlace. He was damp with sweat, but he didn't notice anyone staring at him, a good sign.

After Klein left, Stone had gone to the lawyer's back yard, where he took a long shower, brushed his teeth and shaved. He put on a new set of clothes, shedding his old ones straight to the trash. He walked away feeling presentable enough to go to the bookstore.

Other than the local convenience store, where the owner had learned to tolerate him, and the public library, where tolerating the homeless comes with the territory, Stone hadn't been inside a building in such close proximity to so many people in years — unless you counted the jail.

As soon as he stepped through the doors of the bookstore, he expected to be tapped on the shoulder by a security guard and escorted back to the street. Instead, a young woman with an employee name tag walked up and smiled.

"May I help you find something, sir?"

He was disoriented for a second by the question.

"Poetry," he finally replied.

He took the big elevator to the second floor and felt the air conditioning drying his sweat. But that wasn't why he had goose bumps.

He walked to the poetry section, steeling himself to the possibility that the books wouldn't be there. After all, it was only poetry, the lowest rung on the commercial ladder of publishing. It wasn't as if he was looking for a legal thriller that had been turned into a movie starring Denzel Washington, Tom Cruise or Gene Hackman.

It was only a slender book of poetry, an ephemeral web of ruminations on the human condition that cast a very small shadow on the marketplace of the written word. And yet, there it was. He ran his fingers over the spines of the books, slowing as he reached the R's, and stopping on the one with the moss green dust jacket.

He picked up a copy of the book and traced its perimeter with his fingers.

"Will that be all?" the cashier asked him minutes later as he paid for the book, surprised that it ate up one his $20 bills and part of the other.

He walked outside the store and up to the first trash can he saw. He knew he'd have to throw out the dust jacket. The name on the cover, Marcus Rockman, wouldn't give him away. But the photo on the dust jacket might.

He opened the book to look at the photo on the back flap, surprised to see the confident face that gazed back. Although it had been taken only three years ago, it seemed like another lifetime.

By now, nobody seemed to know or care what had happened to Marcus Rockman, author of seven collections of poetry that garnered more praise than cash. It had been nearly 20 years ago that his first collection had been called "an auspicious debut" by *The New York Times*. But it was this collection, *Word Silo*, his last, that was the most widely read.

"The final volume of the poet laureate that never was," the dust jacket proclaimed.

Marcus Rockman had disappeared without a trace, leaving everything behind in what was widely believed to be a suicide — not an altogether surprising final act for a man in his line of work.

Rockman's disappearance, he suspected, may have helped keep the book in the marketplace, perhaps even more so than the merits of its writing. And as he looked at the dust jacket, he wondered whether throwing it away was even necessary.

Did he even remotely resemble the photo anymore?

Sure, the facial features were the same. But there was something lost in his eyes now and something different about the underlying flesh in his face. He had become a different person, not by cosmetic changes to his facial features, but by the subterranean changes that were like a system of tangled roots strangling everything above them.

He discarded the dust jacket anyway, just to be safe. Besides, he liked the book better this way, showing only its bare, gray hardcover spine to the world and letting the words inside do all the talking.

He walked quickly back toward Belvedere. He wanted to make sure the book was in place before the kids got out of school.

◼

As he mowed her lawn later that day, he kept his eyes on the western horizon, which went from gray to purple. He could sense the shift of wind and knew that rain wasn't far away.

He was emptying the grass catcher when he saw her coming out the back door toward him. She stopped about 15 feet away.

"Can I ask you to do me a favor?" Pinky said.

A bolt of lightning cracked nearby.

"Sure."

The big drops started coming down now. He looked at her, not moving, letting the drops hit him.

"Let's get out of the rain," she said, running into the opened garage.

He followed her, dragging the mower with him.

A moment later, the sky opened up, and the rain came down in sheets, sending a breeze of cool air and fine mist into the garage.

A line from an Edna St. Vincent Millay sonnet popped into his head:

"But the rain is full of ghosts tonight that tap and sigh . . . Upon the glass, and listen for reply."

He said it softly, not looking at her, listening to the rain.

"I had a rat problem here last night, and my husband — well, he was supposed to take care of it this morning and trim those tree branches that are overhanging the roof," she said. "But, as usual, he has proven to be undependable."

She told him about what the exterminator had said. That rats climb trees, and if the tree branches overhang a roof, they will explore there. And so the rat that emerged from her toilet most likely started out on her roof and fell through a toilet vent pipe that should have been screened but probably wasn't.

"I just don't think I want to go through another night here, listening for splashes coming from the toilet," she said.

He was thinking about that sonnet still, the one with the rain that listens for reply. It was a lament, he now recalled, ending with the lines, *"I cannot say what loves have come and gone . . . I only know that summer sang in me . . . A little while, that in me sings no more."*

He could see her looking at him, and he wondered for a moment if he had been thinking aloud.

"I bought some screening, and there's a saw in the garage and a ladder."

"OK."

The rain was letting up already.

"Thanks," she said. "I've got to pick up my daughter from school now."

She hesitated, considering whether to wait for the rain to stop. Then she turned to him.

"We've never really been formally introduced," she said. "My name is Pinky."

She held out her hand to him, and he took it for a second. Summer sang in him, a distant, tentative song. And he marveled at its return.

"Mark," he said.

A half-hour later, Mark Stone was on her roof. He had fastened the screen onto the opened vent pipe and was sawing the last of the overhanging branches when he heard a car pull up. He didn't recognize the car or the man who got out of it, a tall, handsome man with a mane of blond hair. Stone turned to get a better look and in that instant lost his footing on the rain-slick barrel tiles.

He slid on his belly down the pitched roof, heading over the side, unable to grab anything that would stop his fall.

When Pinky drove home, her daughter was the first to spot Travis Plum. He was walking around the side of her house, looking in her windows and talking on a cellphone.

"There's the prince, Mommy," Luna had said.

Pinky hadn't heard a peep from Travis since leaving a message on his machine at 2 that morning. He wasn't in the gym at 9, as he said he would be, and she had gone from being merely curious to disappointed to seriously miffed.

"Just go inside, honey," Pinky told her daughter. "I'll be right there."

Travis saw her as she pulled in the driveway. He quickly finished his call, put the cellphone in his pocket and walked toward Pinky, all smiles.

"There you are," he said. "I was worried about you."

"Since when?" Pinky said, a little frostily. "I called about 15 hours ago."

"I didn't hear your message until just now, and I came right over," he said, all innocence. "I must have had the ringer off on my answering machine."

"And the gym?"

"Didn't you get my message?" he asked. "I left it with the girl at the front desk. I had a Scripps meeting this morning. I completely forgot about it when I told you yesterday I'd meet you at the gym."

"Oh, Travis," Pinky said, starting to feel foolish again.

"So what's the emergency?" he said. "You OK?"

"Yes," she said. "It's been taken care of. I have somebody who is —" She looked around, seeing the ladder but nobody on the roof.

"Where is he?"

"Where's who?" Travis said.

That's when she noticed there was something wrong with the ficus shrubs, not 10 feet from where they were standing. She looked a little closer and saw Mark Stone sprawled in the middle of her bushes.

He wasn't moving.

17
Mysterious ways

When Mark Stone slid off the roof, he didn't have far to fall before he hit the thick bushes. Even so, it knocked the wind out of him and sprained his right ankle.

He stayed there, gazing up at the gray sky, listening to the conversation between Pinky and this man she called Travis. Something wasn't adding up.

Then Pinky saw Mark lying there, and she and Travis got him out of the bushes and sat him down on the back lawn.

"I'm going to call 911," Pinky said.

"No," Mark said. "I'm OK. It's just a sprain."

"I'll get ice," Pinky said, already scooting inside.

Mark looked up at Travis, thinking about what he had heard Travis saying on the cellphone. Mark had heard enough of Travis' end of the conversation to know that the man who told his real girlfriend, "Gotta hang, babe, she's here," as Pinky's car pulled up obviously regarded Pinky as "business."

What sort of business, Stone had no idea.

"You look a little dazed," Travis told him while Pinky was in the house.

"You lied to her about last night," Mark said.

Travis smiled and squatted down, looking at Mark's swollen ankle.

"You'd better watch your step in the future," he told Mark, giving him the impression he was talking about more than merely falling off a roof.

Pinky returned with a plastic bag of ice, followed moments later by Luna, who opened the back door with the breathless announcement, "Daddy's here!"

"Oh, no," Pinky said.

When Cosmo The Lawn King walked down the driveway and into the back yard, he clearly didn't expect to see what he saw. His wife was with two men: the homeless guy who did her lawn and some blond Adonis dressed in disco clothes.

Cosmo looked down at Mark, who had a bag of ice on his ankle.

"Don't tell me," Cosmo said. "He fell off the frickin' roof."

He looked at Pinky.

"I told you I would trim those branches," he said. "You didn't have to rely on an amateur."

Then he looked at Travis, and said, "Are the Bee Gees auditioning for a replacement?"

Pinky stepped in.

"Travis, this is my estranged husband, Cosmo."

"Not as strange as some of the sights around here," Cosmo said.

Travis had a bemused look.

"You're letting quite a gal go," he said.

"How would you know?" Cosmo said.

Luna, who had been silent until now, said, "That's Mommy's boy-friend."

Pinky looked away.

Travis put his arm around her. "That's right," he said.

But she stiffened, and when Mark Stone tried to stand, she extricated herself from the brewing playground theatrics to help him get to his feet.

"I'm sorry for all of this," she told him. "I should have waited for my husband to show up."

Stone's mind was racing. He wanted to tell her not to trust Travis, but he couldn't do it now. So he settled for a cryptic warning.

"Be careful," he told her.

"Oh, don't worry, I'm not going to get on the roof," she said, misunderstanding his warning. "Cosmo will get that last branch."

He was about to say something else, but Travis was suddenly there.

"This might be a good time for me to leave for a little while," he said to Pinky. "How about I give this gentleman here a ride?"

"Oh, that's so considerate of you, Travis."

"Sure, hon," he said, and then put a hand on Mark's shoulder. "C'mon, Hop-along. Let's go."

Mark Stone hobbled to the front yard.

"I can walk," he told Travis.

"Not on that ankle," he said. "C'mon, get in the car."

So he did. As they drove down the block, the car passed Charlie, who was walking home from school. Even at 20 miles an hour, Stone could clearly see the gray spine of his poetry book in the boy's hand.

"Just take me to Belvedere," he said.

Travis drove in silence for a while, but Stone could tell he had something to discuss. Finally, Travis turned to look at him.

"So what's your story? Drugs? Alcohol? Mental illness?"

Stone shrugged, "We all have secret lives."

"Is that so?"

Travis pulled his car into the lot of the convenience store near the intersection of Georgia Avenue.

"Wait here for a second," he said.

Five minutes later, Travis walked back to the car with a brown paper bag. "A present," he said, handing the bag to Stone. It was a quart bottle of Thunderbird wine.

"Aren't you going to say thanks?"

Stone was going to say that he didn't drink. But maybe that wasn't the right approach.

"Thanks," he said, unscrewing the cap and forcing himself to take a swig.

"There's more where that came from," Travis said. "As long as me and you have an understanding."

"And what's that?"

"You just stay out of my business."

Stone nodded, then made himself take another long pull from the bottle of cheap wine.

"Excellent," Travis said, taking a $10 bill out of his pants pocket and tossing it on Stone's lap. "Looks like you're a little thirsty. Have a nice, big bender on me."

Stone stuffed the money in his shirt pocket and stepped out of the car.

He stood there until Travis had disappeared down Belvedere. Then he limped to the side of the building and poured the rest of the Thunderbird on the ground.

That night, Jake called Pinky at about 9.

"Can you come out and play?" he asked.

"Well, I'm not seeing Travis tonight if that's what you're asking," she said.

"Good," Jake said.

"Good?"

"I mean for our plan," he said. "I have the night off, Craig's on duty at the fire station, and there's nothing but repeats on TV. This would be a perfect night to launch your offensive."

"And what offensive is that?"

"Project Gayification," Jake said. "Don't tell me you've forgotten already."

Project Gayification. That was Jake's name for launching Pinky Mulligan as the gay-friendly Realtor in Pelican Park.

"Do you have your newsletter done yet?"

Actually, she had just been stacking copies of it on her dining room table and admiring their glossy, professional look. "Pinky's Perspective" was a four-page newsletter filled with homeowner tips and sales information about homes in Pelican Park. It was printed in color and featured photos of the four homes in the community that Pinky now represented. It also had a portrait of Pinky and her very own column — this first one was about the joys of living in Pelican Park.

"I've got the newsletter," she said.

"Then all you need are your dancing shoes."

"I need to check Luna's homework and then pick up Charlie at 9:30," she said. "I could be ready to go by 10. Is that too late?"

"Is 10 o'clock too late? Oh, my, you breeders really have lost touch with the world."

"Maybe I'll ask Sindee if she wants to break away for a couple of hours and come with us," Pinky said.

"Oh, they'll love Sindee in Lake Worth," Jake said.

"What's in Lake Worth?"

"Tonight just happens to be a big night for lesbian billiards."

■

Pinky had driven by The Holy Blood of the Everlasting Redeemer Church plenty of times but had never gone inside. She parked her car in the small dirt lot at the side of the church. As soon as she stepped out of the car, she could hear music spilling out of the church.

She heard the thumping of drums, a rich carpet of organ chords and the sound of many voices. But mostly she heard the familiar sound of her son's electric guitar, wailing and clawing its way to search for a musical toehold in the mountain of sound around it.

She walked through the main doors and spotted Bishop Crumley sitting in one of the back pews. She sat down next to him, and for some time, they listened in silence as the band and choir worked out the kinks in *Oh Happy Day.*

"So how's the guitar player, Bishop Crumley?"

"For with God, nothing will be impossible," he said. "Luke 1:37."

"That bad?"

"Not bad. Just different. And I suspect it has less to do with God and more to do with a singer in the choir. Second row, third from the left."

"The girl with the red blouse?"

"My daughter, Bea."

Pinky looked at Bishop Crumley, unable to hide her surprise.

"You mean . . .?"

"I been sitting here watching. That boy of yours is spending more time looking at her than the music in front of him. And she's lookin' back."

"I had no idea."

"My son, Terrell, told me, but I didn't believe him. So I came here to see for myself."

They sat in silence, listening and watching.

"He's never had, I mean, you know, any interest in . . ."

"Neither has she."

The rehearsal was breaking up. The musical director was telling everyone when to show up on Sunday. The musicians were putting away their equipment, and the choir members had descended from the risers. Pinky and Bishop Crumley watched as Bea headed over to Charlie. The boy stood up from putting away his guitar, turned to her and smiled.

A moment later, he was taking the guitar back out of his case and showing it to her, eventually strapping it on her and showing her the fingerings for a chord.

She strummed. He nodded.

"Well," said Pinky. "It looks as if you'll have some new parishioners on Sunday."

"We start at 10 sharp," Bishop Crumley said.

"Should I bring anything?" Pinky asked.

"You got a tambourine?"

"No."

"I didn't think so."

Pinky stood up to leave.

"I'd better go corral my son," she said. "Jake Fisher is taking me and Sindee out tonight to shoot pool with lesbians."

"You'll be in my prayers," he said.

"See you Sunday, Calvin."

She walked down the length of the pew, but the bishop's next words stopped her before she reached the center aisle.

"Maybe I was wrong," Bishop Crumley said. "Maybe this is the

Lord's doing."

Pinky shrugged, then said, "It certainly qualifies as one of those mysterious ways."

She continued to the center aisle and to her son, who was still too distracted to notice her.

18

Cosmo goes fishing

It was nearly 2 a.m. when Pinky, Sindee and Jake drove back to Pelican Park. They were all a little giddy from the evening, which, under the direction of Jake, had turned into a whirlwind tour of four gay and lesbian nightspots.

Pinky left stacks of her real-estate newsletters at the clubs, and the excursion had gone from tentative nervousness to a riotous good time, capping off with the three of them singing and dancing with their hands over their heads to *I Will Survive.*

Jake, who was driving, was talking about other clubs they hadn't visited.

"Project Gayification has only just begun," he said.

"Who's hungry?" Sindee asked from the back seat.

"It won't be easy finding anyplace open at this hour."

"My kitchen is open," Sindee said.

Jake and Pinky looked at each other. Sindee never invited anyone into her house. It was, after all, a place of business for her, rigged with cameras in nearly every room — at least that's what she told people.

"Is that an invitation?" Jake asked.

"I'll whip us up some eggs," Sindee said. "It wouldn't kill my clients to wait another hour."

And so Jake parked at Sindee's house, and the three of them walked in through the back door, which opened directly to the kitchen — and what a kitchen it was.

It had a center island, a double oven and an overhanging rack of enough pots and pans to outfit a restaurant. There were rows of knives and gadgets everywhere. Everything was gleaming and of professional quality.

"Wow," Pinky said.

"Welcome to my sanctuary," Sindee said.

Jake had picked up a propane torch on the counter and looked at Sindee.

"To caramelize the sugar on *crème brulée*," she said.

"Yes, please," he said.

"Some other time," she said. "How about a chorizo-and-sour cream omelet?"

They sat there watching her whip up breakfast, helping themselves to thick slices of her homemade bread and slathering it with her own fruit preserves.

"Bathroom?" Pinky asked.

"Down the hall, second door on the left is the guest bathroom," Pinky said. "It's not wired up. But just about every other place in this house is."

Pinky got up from her stool and walked out of the kitchen.

■

Cosmo The Lawn King had come to the conclusion that the bachelor life wasn't all it was cracked up to be. When his wife moved out, he went through a period of liberation, exhilarated to come and go as he pleased without having to concoct a phony explanation.

He could go to the greyhound track every night if he wished, and he wouldn't have to hide his losses or feel compelled to share his winnings. If he wanted to go to the Bahamas for a weekend of poker, nobody would stop him.

So he went. And he bought new clothes, updated his CD collection and began to hang out in earnest at a variety of watering holes on Atlantic Avenue in Delray Beach.

After he and Pinky sold the house, he moved into a beachfront condo in Boca Raton, a place selected for its twin virtues of accepting Gomez and having an outdoor hot tub by the pool. Cosmo found that an invitation for a late-night dip in the hot tub had frequently done the trick to bring a new bar find home with him.

But after a year of carousing, the faces at the bar all started to look familiar, and he, too, had become less of an enticement — a guy who had left too many footprints in the sand.

The gambling debts, already a problem before, grew larger and started taking a bigger dent out of his lawn-care business, making him feel as if he was spending his days working, not to make money, but to avoid being poor.

His life went from joyous to hollow in that year, surprising him by how quickly and unexpectedly it happened. He tried to change. He went to a Gamblers Anonymous meeting, and he took a stab at trying to settle down.

Deirdre was his first attempt at a steady girlfriend, but that lasted only a month. The luster of their romance tarnished after he learned of her sleep apnea, her membership in a soap-opera fan club and her dislike of dogs, particularly Gomez.

He had gone from party guy to a guy asleep in front of his TV, waking up with a stiff neck in the wee hours of the morning to the sound of a motivational speaker or a guy selling exercise equipment.

When the bar scene became less appealing, he turned to the computer, trying to meet women through the Internet. But there was something unsettling about that for him. He was never quite sure if the person he was online with was actually a woman or of legal age. And the only time he agreed to meet one of these online chatters, she turned out to look about 10 years older than her photo.

He found himself, although he never would admit it, wishing he hadn't screwed up his marriage with Pinky. It messed up his relationship with his kids. That was enough of a reason right there for regret. But the past year had also brought him to a growing awareness of what he'd thrown away.

He had still never met anybody as suitable for him as his wife. After 18 years of marriage, they had become, despite their differences, two pieces of the same person. And despite his so-called liberation from her, he felt increasingly diminished by their separation.

To make matters worse, she was the one who apparently had flourished under the new arrangement. She had gone from victim to victor; from somebody to feel sorry for to somebody to envy.

She had taken that dumpy little house in West Palm Beach and turned it into a fine little home. She'd gone back to her maiden name and resumed her long-lost vocation as a real-estate agent. She made new friends, got the kids settled into new lives and had a little constellation of men hanging around her, including some guy with movie-star looks — a boyfriend, according to Luna.

Maybe this was why Cosmo The Lawn King suddenly felt no desire to rush the divorce proceedings. She was winning, and as long as the divorce wasn't final, the game wasn't over. Their separate lives would still be tethered, even if in legal terms only. She still would technically be a married woman, and he would still be the man she'd have to introduce as her husband, modifying adjectives be damned.

And that left the door open to possibilities and changes of heart that could be acted on quickly. So Cosmo had been more than happy to be awakened in the middle of the previous night by his wife. He had gladly driven the half-hour to West Palm to vanquish the rat in her bedroom.

He wasn't happy to find that neighbor of hers, Santiago Klein, already there. But it was he, her husband, who had gotten the job done while that wimpy lawyer bleated ineffectively for rodent leniency.

And then he had gone back today to trim up the branches off her roof and once again proved his trustworthiness to her. OK, so he told her he'd be there in the morning and didn't show up until late in the afternoon. But still, even though she had two other men over there — that homeless guy and the big blond boyfriend guy — once again, it was still he, her husband, who got the job done.

She couldn't deny him that, even though she didn't invite him to stay for dinner and even though she told him she didn't want to go out on "a date" with him, as he so casually put it.

She was still his wife, he told himself, and she could still adjust her attitude. In the meantime, he ended up on Delray's Atlantic Avenue again, spending most of the night at the bar at Mano a Mano and coming home alone, hungry and already feeling the beginnings of a hangover.

He microwaved a burrito and sat in front of his computer, typing in the Web address to see what this other woman he was seeing — in only the most literal of sense of the word — was up to.

■

Pinky finished in the bathroom and started to walk back to the kitchen, but curiosity got the best of her. She saw the soft glow of lights coming from some other rooms of the house, so she took a little detour, going through the living room, the den and finally peeking into another room, where a large waterbed dominated. Sindee's bedroom.

She took a few steps inside and stood there, taking in the décor.

■

"There you are," said Cosmo The Lawn King, when his room-to-room search of Sindee's house revealed the woman standing with her back to him in her bedroom.

He had heard about this Web site from another lounge lizard and was in his second month of membership. At first, he couldn't imagine he'd be interested.

"You mean, she isn't doing anything?" he had said, when told about the *www.iseesultrysindee.com* site.

"No," the guy at the bar said. "She just hangs around her house, vacuuming, watching TV, taking showers, sleeping, and you get to watch it all. It's like being a peeping Tom in the privacy of your own home."

"What's the big deal?" he had asked.

"You never know what she's doing, whether she's even there or not," the guy said. "It's like fishing."

Cosmo thought he'd try it once and then have a story to tell to somebody else. But he found himself joining and wondering at odd times of the day what Sindee was doing.

And now he was wondering again, surprised to see that she wasn't in bed at 2 in the morning but standing in her room with her clothes on. Another first. And there was something different about her hair. It didn't look like Sindee. It looked like . . . another woman. It was another woman.

"Oh, baby," Cosmo said. "Yes, yes. You naughty girl."

Cosmo had never seen anybody but Sindee in her bed, and now the thought of Sindee and this other woman was starting to make Cosmo think this drab little evening of his was going to turn out all right after all.

He had gone fishing and hooked a big one.

"Hee hee," he said to Gomez, who looked up at him and his half-eaten burrito. "Looks like we're in luck tonight."

Then he watched as Sindee walked into the bedroom. The two women had their backs to the camera, but Cosmo was sure this second woman was Sindee. And when she walked up and put her arm around the first woman's shoulders, Cosmo couldn't contain his glee.

"It's showtime, Gomez!"

Sindee walked up to Pinky and put her arm around her shoulder.

"Sorry, I couldn't help but be nosy," Pinky said.

"What would you think of pale yellow on the walls?" Sindee said. "I'm getting tired of this shade of blue."

"I saw a soft pumpkin color in this month's *Better Homes & Gardens*," Pinky said. "I cut it out."

"Show me, but meanwhile, the eggs are ready."

They turned around to walk out of the room, and that's when Pinky looked up and saw the camera mounted on the ceiling. It was staring at her with its operating light glowing like a red eye.

Sindee smiled.

"Sorry, fellas," she said. "I'll make it up to you later."

Cosmo The Lawn King watched as Sindee and her girlfriend turned around and faced the camera. The girlfriend looked up, and in an instant, Cosmo's mood switched from anticipation to dismay.

"Pinky!" he said.

Gomez made his move, snatching the burrito from Cosmo's hand. His owner was too absorbed to notice, still struggling to process this new information.

"Pinky's turned into a switch-hitter!"

19

More than friends

Over the next two months, Pinky Mulligan's world seemed to settle down — not completely, but enough to feel a sense of calm she had lacked for a long time.

Her real-estate business had taken hold in Pelican Park. Her pink yard signs sprouted on every block, causing Marvin Mallow's attitude to transition from disdain to something akin to fear.

"Good morning, Ms. Mulligan," he said to her over tepid eggs at a Chamber of Commerce breakfast. "I believe I may have something for you."

Pinky thought he meant a new property.

"That's nice, Marvin," she said. "Thank you."

"My son and I had a long discussion the other day, and we've come to the conclusion it may be time to add a junior sales agent to the firm," he said.

"I hope you find somebody," Pinky said.

"Why, Ms. Mulligan. I think we already have. I believe your name came up as a possibility."

"Really?" Pinky said. "I'm flattered."

"Then you'll consider it?"

"Absolutely not."

Marvin's fake smile disappeared.

"I believe you're making a big mistake, madam."

"We'll see, Marvin," she said, leaving him there in the buffet line.

Pinky felt her life had a rhythm again, just like it had when she was living in Boca Raton. She found another yoga class and made time every day for a trip to the gym. Just getting that daily shot of endorphins again was like a transfusion for her.

People in the neighborhood were getting to know her, and she was getting to know them. She became the new secretary of the Pelican Park Homeowners Association and main proponent of the effort to spruce up the entryway signs to the neighborhood. And as a member of the motto committee, she had suggested the name, "Pelican Park — A Comfortable Community."

That's how she felt now. Comfortable. It had been so long, she'd almost forgotten what comfortable felt like.

Her kids seemed to have fallen into comfortable routines, as well. Luna befriended a neighborhood girl named Gabriela and came home every day, announcing some new Spanish word she had learned.

"Pass the *pan y mantequilla, por favor,*" she'd say at the dinner table, pointing to the bread and butter.

"Speak English," Charlie would say, as he handed over the bread.

"Gracias," Luna would answer.

Charlie, who still didn't let Pinky in on most of his life, seemed happy, too. He traveled every day back and forth to school with Bishop Crumley's two kids and had become a regular member of The Holy Blood of the Everlasting Redeemer musical ensemble.

"What's wrong with Charlie?" Cosmo asked Pinky, after returning his son to Pelican Park on a Saturday night. "He's always in a rush to get back here."

"He's sweet on a girl," Pinky said.

"Really?" Cosmo said.

"See for yourself."

The next morning, Cosmo sat dumbfounded in the rear pew of The Holy Blood of the Everlasting Redeemer Church. It was quite a shock, first of all, to see his son up behind the altar, playing guitar with an all-black choir and band, and stealing glances at the pastor's seventh-grade daughter.

It was a double shock for Cosmo The Lawn King to see his wife take a tambourine out of her purse and start shaking it during one of the hymns. And it was a triple shock to see Sindee Swift sitting there, in the flesh, next to his wife.

"Cosmo, this is my best friend and neighbor, Sindee," Pinky said.

"Hi," Sindee said, shaking Cosmo's hand, a hand that already had a connection to her in ways he dared not reveal.

Cosmo was hoping he wasn't staring too hard, but he had never seen her in three dimensions, and in that instant, he was so envious of his wife, he failed to be surprised that his son had become smitten by a black girl.

"Are you two . . . more than friends?" he asked Pinky after the church service.

"What?"

"You and Sindee," he said. "You know what I mean. Let's be adults here."

Pinky just laughed, and thinking back on it, Cosmo found her to be suspiciously unresponsive to his question. He doubled up his viewings of Sindee's Web site to monitor the situation, and he couldn't tell whether the churning in him was a sense of dread or anticipation.

But he never saw his wife again on the Web site.

That's because Pinky was seeing Travis. She was still showing him houses in the neighborhood, but he hadn't made an offer yet.

"I'm just waiting for the right one," he told her.

Pinky didn't mind. Actually, she enjoyed this time with Travis the most, because he was always full of good ideas and great conversation. And this was when they usually made plans to see each other at night.

It had become steady but not serious. She was content to see him maybe two nights a week and meet him at the gym on a couple of other weekly occasions.

It had developed into a comfortable relationship for Pinky, even though Jake continued to make cryptic digs at Travis.

"He lacquers his nails," he finally told Pinky one day.

"So what are you saying, he's gay?" Pinky asked.

"No," Jake said. "My gaydar is one of the best this side of Old Northwood."

"So what then?"

"I just don't picture a microbiologist going for a manicure, that's all."

"I wouldn't think you'd be the person to stereotype others," Pinky said.

"Maybe you're right," Jake said, dropping the subject.

Pinky's renewed sense of calm even allowed her to relax around Carl LaCerda, the West Palm Beach police detective who still found reasons to drop by and talk to her.

Pinky had come to believe that LaCerda was just a harmless flirt, not the worst thing in the world for a woman to endure as she neared her 43rd birthday.

"There's been a string of home burglaries in the past couple months," LaCerda told her as he stopped in front of her home one afternoon while she was taking groceries out of her car.

"Yes, that's all Uncle Sherman has been talking about," Pinky said.

Uncle Sherman, who monitored the police frequencies, had delivered a 10-minute recitation via speakerphone on the subject during the last homeowners association meeting. He had detailed every home burglary and itemized each mode of forced entry and each item stolen.

"You haven't seen any suspicious characters in the neighborhood lately, have you?" the detective asked.

"No," Pinky said. "Can't say that I have."

"How about that peeping Tom?" the detective said. "He ever give you any trouble again?"

Pinky hesitated.

"I think you have things wrong there, detective," Pinky said.

Pinky wasn't quite sure what to make of Mark Stone, but she knew he wasn't a pervert. He was almost painfully shy around her. He still mowed her lawn on a weekly basis, weeded her garden and toiled happily there until she told him to go away.

She had stopped being afraid of him but hadn't gotten comfortable talking to him, either.

"Are you OK?" she had said to Stone when he showed up with the mower about a week after falling off her roof.

He seemed confused by the question.

"Your ankle," she said.

"Oh," he said. "It's fine."

But he walked with a little limp, and he acted as if he wanted to tell her something.

"How about you? You OK?" he finally asked.

He looked at her with searching eyes, the same eyes that scared her when she had looked at them through the two-way glass of a police lineup. But now she saw something different. Something almost needy. Something far too embracing. And it made her feel oddly adrift and unsure of herself.

"Fine, fine," she said.

He started to say something else, but she pretended that she heard the phone ringing inside.

"Gotta take that call," she said and walked quickly back inside, wondering to herself if maybe she should have less contact with him.

She didn't want to lead him on. He was, for crying out loud, a street guy.

The next time Santiago Klein stopped by to pick up money from her, the lawyer said: "I don't know why we're even doing this anymore, Pinky. You can certainly pay Mark yourself."

"I'd rather still do it this way," Pinky said, handing him two $20 bills.

"He's an intelligent, gentle man," the lawyer said. "You've got nothing to be frightened about."

"Then why is he homeless?"

"Ah," Klein said. "You've asked the jackpot question."

■

The jackpot question for Pinky's son was to figure out the identity of the person who was corresponding with him via messages left at the phone booth on the corner of Lake Avenue and Belvedere Road.

Charlie Hope had gotten into the habit of dropping off envelopes. It started out as schoolwork but had gradually turned to long, diary-like missives about his life.

There's this girl I like, he would write. *And sometimes, I'm not sure what to say to her, and her big brother's always around anyway. And I feel like such a dork because I basically only know about stuff that she doesn't know about, and if I talk about like, Cobain, she like looks at me like I'm talking Spanish or something.*

Charlie would find the reply, always printed in green ink in neat block letters.

JUST BE YOURSELF.

Who are you? Charlie would write back, after realizing that "Anon" was just a shortened form of "anonymous."

But there was never an answer. So Charlie invented his own name for his discreet correspondent, identifying him as Agent Booth. The longer this arrangement went on, the more Charlie wanted to know who Agent Booth really was.

One day, he got an idea. While walking home from school, he put another envelope in the phone booth on Belvedere, then told Bea and Terrell to walk on home without him.

"What are you going to do?" Terrell asked.

"I'm going do some surveillance," Charlie said.

"I'm staying with Charlie," Bea said.

"No, you're not," her big brother said.

Bea pitched a fit, but in the end, she obeyed her brother.

Charlie watched his friends walk away, then he crossed the street to the abandoned gas station, looking for a spot to hide out in view of the phone booth.

He was so excited about the prospect of discovery that he didn't notice Ray-Ray, who was leaving the convenience store with his posse. The bully stopped for a moment, seeing Charlie standing alone on the sidewalk with his protector nowhere in sight.

A big smile came to Ray-Ray's face, as he loped with his posse down the sidewalk, a bouncing shuffle of trouble that Charlie didn't notice until they were only a few steps away.

"Hey, Boca boy," Ray-Ray said.

Charlie's first impulse was to run, but he knew it was already too late.

20

The life he never lived

Mark Stone had been watching it all, watching as Charlie put the envelope in the phone booth, then watching him say goodbye to his friends.

When the teenager crossed the street to the abandoned gas station, he walked straight toward Stone, who sat on the milk crate by the back fence. But the boy hadn't seen him there.

It was the homeless man who first saw Ray-Ray, and quickly figured out what was about to occur.

"Oh, no, little Boca boy doesn't have his protection," Ray-Ray said, as his posse slipped behind Charlie, cutting off his escape route.

Charlie started to backpedal, but the other boys just pushed him toward Ray-Ray.

Mark knew he'd have to think of something fast. He felt panic rising, but this time something was compelling him to rise from his milk crate, and to come up with words, not for their beauty, but for their usefulness in this flesh-and-blood world.

"Ya buncha hooligans!" he yelled, staggering toward them in his impression of a crazy drunk.

He grabbed an empty Winn-Dixie shopping cart that had been abandoned nearby, figuring it might come in handy.

"Get the dickens off my property!" he said, as he wheeled the cart closer to the cluster of five boys.

His approach surprised Ray-Ray and his friends. They were put off by the demeanor of the familiar homeless man who had always been another meek victim of theirs. They laughed at him now, which seemed to get him more angry.

"You're trespassing on my property!"

"Yo, homeless dude," Ray-Ray said. "Go back to your bottle, or you gonna regret it."

Stone was stalling for time. He needed to hold them there for a few more seconds, which was how long it would take him to walk with the cart another 10 feet. So he let the words that came so effortlessly to him flow out of his mouth, this time in a fake-drunk reading.

"My regrets," Stone said, *"come to me in elastic dreams, in memories long-covered by the weeds of time, in the faces of those I've touched, and those I would have touched in the life I never lived."*

Ray-Ray and his posse howled with laughter, but Charlie's brow furrowed.

"Dude's trippin' on angel dust," one of the boys said.

Stone stopped, stooping and pretending to vomit. It had the effect of making them laugh again at him, and then turn their attention back to Charlie. Just what Stone wanted.

He felt his breathing quicken. It was now or never. He lunged, crashing into the pack of boys, making sure to maneuver the cart between Charlie and Ray-Ray, then stumbling back in one sweeping motion, to get his body between Charlie the others, who instinctively moved away from the homeless man.

For a second, he could sense everyone's surprise, and he could only hope that Charlie saw that this was his only opening. He did. By the time Stone turned around, Charlie was already sprinting down the sidewalk, his tormenters too disoriented to catch him.

Mark Stone nearly smiled. But he knew what was coming next, and it wasn't going to be pleasant. The four boys turned their attention to him now. They weren't laughing anymore.

Five minutes later, his mouth full of grit, his head bloodied, he thought his ordeal was over. But then he saw Ray-Ray flash a truly evil smile, and even though Stone's eyes were already closing from the swelling, he could see the shiny blade of the knife appear in the teenager's hand.

And before the first wave of coolness washed over him, Mark Stone heard his own voice whisper its confession.

"I'm sorry, Celia."

◾

Celia Waverly was the first girl he had ever loved. They were 19. He was home from college for the summer, and she had never left home. They'd gone to high school together but never really knew each other until that summer when he was shucking clams, peeling shrimp and cleaning squid in the kitchen at Porky's, a seafood restaurant on Long Island.

Celia was a waitress there, and he might never have gotten to know her if he hadn't started smoking cigarettes his sophomore year of college, a habit he later discontinued when he realized that while smoking was frequently the practice of many a tortured genius, it wasn't a requirement.

He'd find Celia out behind the restaurant, sitting on a wooden crate by the dock, blowing smoke toward the shimmering bay.

It was a romantic spot, if you discounted the rotting fish smell coming from the nearby Dumpster and the constant briny aroma he wore like cologne that whole summer. He got to know her during these smoke breaks as they filled in the awkward moments between puffs with idle conversation.

"God, I wish I could go away to college," she had said.

"It's not all it's cracked up to be," he lied.

For Celia, this was it. Bay Shore. The waitressing job. She was saving her tips to buy a used car, but for that summer, she rode her bike to the restaurant, parking it out there by the Dumpster and then pedaling it home after the restaurant closed.

"Let me give you a ride home," he said one night. "It's not safe riding your bike like that in the dark. We can put it in the trunk of my dad's car."

And that's how it started. The smoke breaks led to the rides home, which led to stopping for a beer on the way home, which led to the back seat of his dad's car and eventually her bedroom when her parents weren't home.

It was, looking back on it, the best time of his life, although he was still too foolish to imagine that the best part of life isn't what you think you need to achieve, but in enjoying what you have.

She visited him at Dartmouth College that fall, and later, around Valentine's Day. The next summer, he came home again to work at Porky's, where she was still a waitress who rode a bike to work.

By then, his head was full of big ideas, of Frost and Whitman, of Pound and Blake, of Dostoevsky and Shakespeare, of Camus and Thoreau and W. Somerset Maugham.

A professor had already pulled him aside and told him, "You have a voice, a talent that deserves nurturing." And he had already had a couple of his poems and stories published in literary journals.

"What's next?" Celia Waverly asked him one night, as they lay tangled in her bed, their fish restaurant clothes piled on the floor in a reeking heap and Celia's high-school graduation mortarboard tassel hanging from the headboard.

That second summer was slipping away, and he knew an honest answer called for telling her about his dream to travel Europe for a year or two and then go to graduate school.

"Maybe you can visit campus again in October," he said.

"Maybe," she said, and he could hear the defeat in her voice, and it tugged on his heart, because at that time, he hadn't yet fully felt the walls closing in around him there in her room. He was still swirling in the delusions of the flesh, and of the discovery and wonder that animates every courtship that's worth a damn.

"Maybe we can get married," he heard himself say, "someday."

The words hung there for a moment, and then he felt her squeeze him, and when she spoke next, her voice was small, but crushing in its hopefulness.

"Maybe," she whispered.

It wasn't until two months later that she told him she was pregnant, an announcement that she had played out in her mind a million times, but never in the way it was eventually delivered.

She had come to visit him at Dartmouth during the first semester of his senior year, and they both said they had "big news" for the other.

"You go first," he had said, as they sat on a bench in the middle of campus on a day cold enough to make the vapor of each other's breath collide in a common cloud.

"No, you," she said.

"OK, I have a fellowship," he said.

"What's that?" she asked.

"A year of study. Abroad."

"Abroad?"

"Paris."

"I'm pregnant."

"I get a stipend and . . . What?"

"Three months."

"No."

"Yes," she said, holding both his hands, waiting for him to hug her.

But instead, he just sat there, and she could see his mind working rather than his heart.

"So that's early? Right?" he said. "I mean, three months is like no big deal . . . if it's . . . if it needs to be . . . fixed."

She hung her head.

"I thought you'd be happy."

"Celia," he said, "Don't you see, I can't . . ."

But she had already started to walk away. He followed her.

"I'll pay for everything," he said. "And you can come visit me in Paris next summer."

She got on the next bus to New York.

The next few weeks, he called her six or seven times before she picked up the phone. When she did, she told him she didn't need his money, that everything would be "fixed" without his help.

During Christmas break, he returned to Long Island, and looked for her at the restaurant and at her home. But no one answered the door at her house, and the people at Porky's said she had quit.

He wrote her a long letter that winter, explaining how his life had taken a path, and how he had seen those people in Porky's, the couples that came in with kids. And how, while that life was noble, it was too constricting for him. He didn't want to need a full-time job, just for the sake of making ends meet. He didn't want to be a family man. He wanted to be a great man.

He actually wrote that. "I want to be a great man."

He read the letter a second time and sent it. He never got a letter back.

He graduated that spring and went off to France, happily immersing himself in a new world. It was only his sense of smell that occasionally brought him back to those summer nights behind the restaurant with Celia.

He discovered over the next 20 years that he would meet and become attracted to many women — even briefly marrying one — but none of them disquieted his soul like Celia Waverly.

He never knew what became of her until he got a phone call at his university office, a few days before he would have been appointed America's next poet laureate, a selection that would have established his place among the pantheon of the nation's most honored writers.

"Professor Rockman," he said, picking up the phone.

"Marcus Rockman?" the voice said.

"Yes," he said.

It was hard to hear the woman caller. Passing traffic rushed in the background, and it was one of those pay phones that had been slammed down too many times.

"The great man?"

"Who is this?" he shouted.

"Your daughter."

Three years later, Mark Stone, homeless and bleeding, lay on the sidewalk across the street, looking at that very same phone booth where the daughter he never knew had called him.

"I'm sorry, Celia," he said, again, thinking now that he might never find the child who was born — not fixed — when a young poet pursued what he foolishly had thought to be the meaning of life.

21

To freedom

When Pinky Mulligan left the Palm Beach County Judicial Center in West Palm Beach, she had no inkling that the sound of distant sirens racing toward Belvedere Road had any connection to her. She barely noticed them, listening instead to the sound of footsteps rapidly approaching from behind as she walked down the stone steps.

"Pinky, wait up," Cosmo called.

She reached the bottom of the steps and stopped, watching the slightly overweight, uncomfortable-in-his-dress-clothes father of her children huff and puff his way to her.

"Well, if it isn't my ex-husband," she said.

"Free at last."

"Congratulations."

"You, too," he said. "So . . . you going to celebrate?"

"I don't know," Pinky said, unconsciously reaching to straighten the knot in his tie as she had done so many times during their 18-year marriage. "I guess I should. How about you?"

"Absolutely," Cosmo said. "I believe it's required."

They walked to the parking garage together, and for the first time that day weren't flanked by their divorce lawyers.

"So, was it like you expected?" she asked.

"Today? No, not at all."

After a year of legal wrangling, of haggling over alimony and child support, of sorting out Cosmo The Lawn's King's tenuous financial empire, it had ended that afternoon in a courtroom that seemed far too big and empty for the proceeding. The final hearing in their dissolution-of-marriage case took only 10 minutes and played to empty seats and a judge who moved things along quickly and then fled back to his chambers the moment the last paper was signed.

"Me neither," Pinky said.

She nearly added, "I've been through real-estate closings with more emotion," but she didn't trust herself to explain why she had wanted and expected something more visceral than what appeared to be a bloodless business transaction.

They crossed Dixie Highway and entered the parking garage.

"How's the car running?" he asked.

"Fine."

"Good."

They reached her car, and she fumbled for the keys in her purse, finally shaking it up and down and listening for the jangling sound.

"So," he said, "have you had dinner yet?"

"It's 4:30," she said, finding her keys and looking up at him.

"That must be why I'm not hungry," he said.

She still hadn't made a move to put the keys in her car door.

"I'm kind of surprised that Todd isn't here with you," he said.

"Travis."

"Whatever."

"Yeah, whatever."

"That mean you broke up?"

"No, it doesn't mean that."

"Oh, I just thought . . . never mind."

"So, where did you get that tie?" she asked.

"You like it?"

She had realized sometime that afternoon that she was familiar with virtually every bit of her husband's clothing. She remembered the day she went with him to get the suit he wore. And she remembered the three shoe stores she dragged him to before settling on the wingtips he had on. The shirt. The belt. Even his socks had a familiarity to her. But the tie? That was something far too garish and strange. She definitely had nothing to do with that. It made her try to picture Cosmo buying clothes for himself, something she had never stopped to imagine.

"I got it at one of those kiosks in the mall," he said.

She could picture that.

She started to put the keys in her car.

"Pinky," he said.

But when she turned around to look at him, he didn't seem to have anything more to say. A car pulled up, waiting for Pinky's spot. She turned to look at it, then back at Cosmo.

"I need a drink," she said.

"Me too."

She put the keys back in her purse. Cosmo motioned for the waiting car to move on.

He yelled to the driver: "We're not going anywhere after all."

"To freedom," Cosmo said, holding up his martini glass in a toast.

They were sitting at the same restaurant — even the same sidewalk table at that restaurant — where she and Travis had sat the first time they had dinner.

"To freedom," she responded, and they both took a sip.

When the second martini arrived, Cosmo announced it was her turn to make a toast. And it may have been because of the first martini, or it may have been simply the need to peel away some of the artifice of that afternoon, but whatever the reason, Pinky offered the toast she felt most like making.

"To us," she began, "for those good years we had."

She sniffed a little and clinked glasses with Cosmo.

"To us," Cosmo said.

The first martini was enough to make Pinky feel lightheaded. The second one sent her into orbit.

"Let me buy you dinner," Cosmo said after they had drained the second round.

"The kids," Pinky said.

"Call 'em up," Cosmo said. "Isn't there something they can microwave for dinner?"

She called them from her cellphone at the table. Luna answered, and as always, she had lots of questions.

"Why aren't you coming home for dinner, Mommy?"

"I'm busy."

"With Travis?"

"No."

"The gym?"

"I'm with . . . Daddy."

"Oh," Luna said. "Are you fighting?"

"Not yet."

"Can I talk to him?"

Pinky handed the phone to Cosmo.

"Hi honey," he said. "Me and Mommy are having a nice time together."

"You are?" Luna said. "That's, like, so . . . weird."

And it was, because Pinky and her newly minted ex-husband had the most enjoyable meal they'd shared in years. As Pinky scraped away the final remnants of chocolate fondant from her bowl, she looked up at Cosmo, who had long ago removed that hideous tie and was now staring at her with what she saw was unguarded admiration.

"Why couldn't you be like this when we were married?" she asked.

"Why did you marry a fool?" he answered.

"Because he used to rock my world."

"People change."

"I know," she said. "I found out the hard way."

"What I meant," Cosmo said, reaching across the table for her hands, "is that people never stop changing."

She pulled away her hands, but not at first.

And when he walked her back to her car, and a polite goodbye kiss morphed into a long hug and then a real kiss — something they hadn't shared in more than a year — Pinky sighed deeply and asked, "Now what?"

"I know a place," he said.

She followed him in her car to the Knight's Inn on 45th Street, just east of I-95. She waited in the car while he dashed into the lobby and came out dangling a key in his hand, and pumping his other fist in mock triumph.

She wondered how many times he had done this before with someone else when they were married, and it began to sour her mood. But not enough to make her stop following his truck to the back of the motel parking lot.

"Here we are," he said, as she trailed him into the room, closing the door to the sounds of roaring traffic on the nearby highway.

"Can I ask you a question?"

"Please don't," he said, perhaps sensing the sort of thing that might have crossed her mind. "Not tonight."

She was already starting to get a headache from the martinis and the wine at dinner, and the regret of following him here was coming on as surely as the hangover she would have in the morning.

"Maybe this wasn't such a good idea," she said.

"No, no, it will be great," he said. "I'm going to run outside and get some ice."

But as he dashed out of the room with the bucket in his hand, she was thinking more of another kind of machine, one that usually featured photos of women in some exaggerated pose of ecstasy over the ribbed, lubricated and oddly colored contents of the packages vended inside.

Cosmo Hope wasn't anyone she could trust anymore. He was like any other man in her life these days, a possible source of infection, a would-be betrayer, a man with a limited guarantee who couldn't be taken at his word.

They had been fooling themselves all evening, pretending that maybe life hadn't really changed after they had both been traumatized by the cold finality of their divorce.

"Listen, Cosmo," she began when he returned with the bucket of ice, his face full of foolish expectation.

She was still standing in the same spot she had been when he left the room.

"Oh," he said, understanding everything just by the expression on her face and by the way she had remained anchored to that same patch of carpet.

"Everything's different now," she said. "There has to be a promise of something, doesn't there?"

"I still love you, Pinky," he said, the ice starting to make crackling sounds from the bucket he held.

"And I still love you, too, Cosmo," she said. "But not in the way I used to. Which was with everything I had."

"Let's not over-think this, Pinky."

"You can probably still get your money back for the room," she said.

She walked over and kissed him on the cheek.

"I'm sorry for being so conflicted."

"Well, it's understandable," he said, forcing a smile. "You got divorced today."

"To freedom," she said.

"I haven't given up on you, Pinky Mulligan."

"You already have. It's just crossed your mind that it may have been a mistake."

When Pinky got home, she thought her kids were asleep, but as soon as she turned out the light and got in bed, she heard footsteps.

"So how was Daddy?" Luna asked, snuggling next to her mother.

"You should be asleep," Pinky said.

But instead of sending her daughter off to her own bed, Pinky hugged the girl to her and stroked her hair.

"What's the matter, Mommy?"

"Nothing," Pinky answered, barely above a whisper.

"Did you and Daddy have a fight?"

"No, we had a nice evening."

"Better than Travis?"

"Yeah, better than Travis."

"Then why are you sad?"

22
John Doe 77

The next day, Charlie Hope made a point of sticking close to Terrell and Bea Crumley when he walked to and from school. He had let his guard down with Ray-Ray, and it nearly got him pulverized.

"If it wasn't for the crazy homeless guy, I'd have been toast," Charlie told the Crumley kids.

The way Charlie remembered it, the homeless guy didn't actually try to save him from the bullies. He merely made his drunken entrance into the middle of them, and it was Charlie, by his ingenuity alone, who engineered his own escape.

"You should have seen it," he bragged. "In the confusion, I just took off. I never quit running till I got home."

They stopped by the phone booth, but the envelope he had left there was still in its spot, untouched.

And it was still there all the next day and the day after that and the day after that. When a whole week had gone by, and Charlie's secret phone-booth correspondent had yet to pick up or reply to his last envelope, Charlie began to worry.

"Maybe Agent Booth got tired of me," Charlie said to Bea one night on the phone.

Other than Charlie Hope, nobody had counted on Mark Stone to do anything, at least not right away. So his disappearance from Belvedere Road went unnoticed for days.

Santiago Klein never knew for sure when the homeless man came and went from his back yard to take showers and pick up fresh clothes. Pinky Mulligan marked Stone's presence only by the length of her grass, which he mowed on his own erratic schedule. And other than detective Carl LaCerda, nobody at the West Palm Beach Police Department made it a point to monitor the homeless man's situation. And LaCerda himself would go days, even weeks, without checking up on Stone.

The homeless man existed in a netherworld, achieving a kind of invisibility as he lay sprawled on the sidewalk long after the footsteps of Ray-Ray and his posse faded away.

Several cars had passed by, their drivers taking him for a passed-out drunk. If it wasn't for the pool of bright blood that had begun to form around him, he might have gone unnoticed a lot longer than the 20 minutes it took for the first 911 call to be placed.

He arrived at the emergency room at Good Samaritan Medical Center as John Doe 77. The knife wound to his abdomen was substantial, and the loss of blood had put him into shock, but it hadn't pierced any major arteries or organs.

He would live, and because of that, the interest in his wound would be minimal. Nobody would really want to know what happened to John Doe 77. He was just another homeless guy who nearly died from living on the street.

The sad truth was that the world was full of people like him who had been beaten and stabbed for no other reason than the change in their pockets. If he had lived in a waterfront Palm Beach mansion, it would be a different story. There would be an investigation of motives and a list of possible suspects. There would be stories written and broadcast on TV. And some people wouldn't sleep well at night until answers were unearthed.

But the questions here could easily go unanswered, and no one would care. This was just a matter of sewing him up and getting him back on the street as quickly as possible to minimize the drain on taxpayers that people like John Doe 77 create when they require emergency care.

For days, Mark Stone stared at the hospital room's ceiling tiles. The people who came by to see him had jobs to do, and they did them efficiently, changing IV bags, cleaning his wound, delivering his meals. They cared for him but not about him. He was, even with his host of attendants, still alone.

There was a television in his room, suspended by a bracket in the corner, and it was turned on day and night. He hadn't watched television in years, but he couldn't help but watch it now, marveling in its non-stop presentation of a world of products, not ideas; of contrived happy endings and contrived controversy; of love lost and always found, right on schedule.

By the third day, the day he regained his voice, he made the only request he'd make during his weeklong stay.

"Please," he told the nurse, reaching for her as she turned to walk out of the room. "Turn that thing off."

◼

Pinky Mulligan found out about Mark Stone's stabbing through the Pelican Park Homeowners Association. But only in a roundabout way.

The meeting, which was held at the home of Jake Fisher and Craig Shelbourne, featured a discussion about creating a "Home of the Month" designation, which would include a yard sign.

"Well, you'd better chain the blessed thing down," Uncle Sherman boomed from the speakerphone, "or it'll end up getting stolen like everything else around here."

Pinky figured that Uncle Sherman was about to add a racially bigoted addendum to his comment. So she quickly interrupted.

"The important thing is that with a Home of the Month, maybe we'd get more people to take better care of their yards," she said.

Uncle Sherman, who didn't appreciate being interrupted and had one of the more unkempt yards in the neighborhood, shot back: "Oh, I see what this is about. Pinky Mulligan is just trying to drum up some new landscaping clients for Cosmo The Lawn King, her husband."

"That's not true!" Pinky said.

"Hey, hey," Jake said. "Let's be civil here."

Pinky was unusually quiet for the rest of the meeting.

As she was ready to leave, Jake sensed her frustration.

"He's just a crazy old man," Jake said. "Don't take what he says to heart."

"I don't even use Cosmo to do my own lawn," she said.

Craig, who was cleaning up and listening, chimed in, "Who does your lawn, Pinky? It looks nice."

"Actually," she said, "it's a long story, but a homeless guy does it. The guy you see on Belvedere all the time. By the abandoned gas station on the corner of Lake."

"No!" Craig said, suddenly very interested, but not in the way Pinky imagined.

"Yes," she said. "It was through Santiago Klein, who . . ."

"When was the last time you saw that homeless guy?" Craig interrupted.

"I don't know, a week ago, maybe more. Come to think of it, the lawn is due for a cut. If you'd like, I can send him over to your place when he . . ."

That's when she noticed the pained look in Craig's face.

"What?" she said.

"We responded to a call on Belvedere Monday afternoon. I was the EMT on the scene. Your guy, he got stabbed. Pretty bad. We took him to Good Sam."

Charlie Hope was vaguely aware of his mother's return from the homeowners association meeting. He was in his bedroom instant-messaging Bea on his computer while downloading music, so he wasn't really paying attention to the voices coming from the kitchen.

What usually happened was that his mom and Sindee would hang out and talk over bowls of ice cream.

They're back, he IM'd Bea. *I'm going in for ice cream.*

But when he went to the kitchen, his mom and Sindee were just standing there, too intent on whatever they were talking about to reach in the freezer. And there was another neighbor, the manic lawyer, Santiago Klein. They all seemed to be worked up about something, which was par for the course on homeowners association nights.

So Charlie wasn't paying much attention.

"I had no idea," Santiago was saying.

"I wonder if he's still there?" Pinky said.

"There's only one way to find out," Sindee said.

Charlie opened the freezer door.

"Who wants ice cream?"

Nobody answered. Instead, he heard his mother punch three numbers into the kitchen phone and say, "West Palm Beach. Good Samaritan Hospital. The emergency room."

Charlie pulled out the container of Black Jack Cherry.

"What's going on?" he asked breezily.

"You know the homeless guy who cuts your lawn?" Sindee said.

Charlie heard his mother say into the phone, "There was a man in the emergency room Monday afternoon. He was stabbed on Belvedere Road . . ."

Santiago Klein was saying to Sindee, "I should have paid more attention to his comings and goings."

"Don't blame yourself," his neighbor said. "He's an adult."

"I don't even remember the last time I saw him," Klein said.

Charlie's mind raced. He remembered when he last saw the homeless man. It was when Ray-Ray nearly beat Charlie up. Monday afternoon!

"His name is Mark Stone," he heard his mother say.

Charlie wondered now whether Ray-Ray and his posse might have taken out their frustration at letting Charlie get away by attacking the homeless guy. Was Ray-Ray planning to stab Charlie? Did the homeless guy die in his place?

The boy sat down at the kitchen table, going pale.

"Maybe that's him," Pinky said. "Thank you."

Pinky hung up the phone and looked at Sindee.

"A John Doe was brought into the emergency room that day. I'll bet that's him."

"So he's alive?" Santiago said.

"Still in the hospital," Pinky said. "In stable condition."

"We've got to go see him!" Charlie cried out.

The three adults looked at Charlie, his mother noticing him for the first time.

"You need to stay here with your sister," Pinky said.

"Mom!"

"Mom, nothing," Pinky said.

What could he say? That he knew what happened to Mark Stone? He hadn't spoken a word about Ray-Ray or any of this to his mother.

"We'll be back soon," his mother told him. "Meanwhile, have you finished all your homework?"

Without answering, Charlie walked back toward the beaded-curtain entrance to his room. The lawyer was talking as the three adults headed out of the house.

"If only I had done more to get him off the street," Klein was saying to the two women. "If he was a drunk or an addict, it might have been easy to get him in some kind of program."

"I thought all homeless people had addiction issues," Sindee said.

"Not Mark," Klein said. "He doesn't drink or do drugs."

The front door closed, and Charlie couldn't hear their conversation anymore. But he had heard enough. If Mark Stone didn't drink, then he was faking being drunk when he staggered into Ray-Ray and his posse.

Why would he do that? Charlie messaged Bea, after explaining everything he had just learned.

To save you, dummy!!! she messaged back.

Why? Charlie typed back.

But already, there was a dawning in him, a thread of understanding that had begun taking root.

Gotta go now, he typed, then got up from his chair, without even waiting for Bea's reply.

23
April fool

On that day three years before, when his 20-year-old daughter phoned him to announce both her existence and her demands, Marcus Rockman went from being a man about to be appointed as poet laureate, to a man living with a new and unbearable burden. He walked around campus in a daze, eventually returning to his office and closing the door. He pulled a yellow legal pad out of his desk drawer.

"April," he wrote in his meticulous script, stopping there, pondering those five letters for the next half-hour. He had meant to write her a letter, but he had nowhere to send it, and all that spilled out of him was a poem:

My regrets come to me in elastic dreams,
in memories long covered by the weeds of time,
in the faces of those I've touched,
and those I would have touched
in the life I never lived.

My success knows no measure of fame or fortune,
No collection of carefully mined words or
sentiments shared. But only what happens next,
and whether flowers may still grow from a
garden so tragically untended.

He phoned his publisher in New York. His newest collection of poems was in galley form, sitting on his desk, awaiting his final approval.

"There's a new poem," he said, barely listening to the exasperated lecture that erupted on the other end of the line.

"I don't care," Rockman said. "I'll pay for the changes. Just put it in."

The poem, entitled *April*, was the last piece Marcus Rockman published. He failed to show up at the Library of Congress three days later, offering no explanation as to why he declined his selection as poet laureate and its $35,000 annual stipend. Then he walked away from his tenured post at the university.

The apparent emotional breakdown of Marcus Rockman made news, but in the big scheme of things, it was barely a blip, not even registering on the Brad Pitt Breakup Scale of arts-and-entertainment happenings. Poets were, by definition, expected to be tortured souls, and Marcus Rockman fell short of making a spectacular exit: sticking his head in an oven, jumping off a bridge or walking into a river with stones in his pockets — the benchmark achievements in his field.

So, the wider world knew next to nothing of Marcus Rockman, although his disappearance did nudge the sales of his final book of poems, *Word Silo*, and created a special interest among hard-core poetry buffs to that final poem, *April*, which, as the story went, was the author's lament to the writing life he abandoned.

Graduate students dissected the poem, its title widely assumed to be the month of the year, mostly due to the garden reference in the last line. It was, they mostly concluded, the work of a frustrated man who'd lost faith in his work and in the purpose of a life in words.

April, rather than being a month of new growth, had become a dead spring, a kind of continuation of winter. The "what happens next" line was assumed to be a reference to the hereafter, the next world, and reason to assume that his disappearance would turn out to be a suicide.

Nobody ever did find the body of Marcus Rockman at the bottom of a remote canyon, on the bank of a river or in a seedy motel room. Nevertheless, *Word Silo* sold nearly twice as many copies as any of his previous collections of poems, causing Rockman's publisher to comment drunkenly during a Manhattan dinner party that all poets should consider suicide as a marketing strategy.

Interest in what happened to Marcus Rockman died quickly. It didn't take long for him to become a curious footnote, as each year went by, and yet another poet laureate was appointed, and another batch of Oregon students came and went without him.

Marcus Rockman had faded into oblivion to everyone except for one 14-year-old boy in West Palm Beach, who sat up on this night, leafing quickly through the pages of *Word Silo* until he found that final poem.

For, on this night, Charlie Hope had figured out what no one else had: that Marcus Rockman had become Mark Stone, that a renowned poet from Oregon had made the diagonal trek across America to Florida, becoming a homeless man living at an abandoned gas station on Belvedere Road.

And that it was Stone, this homeless man whom he saw without really seeing, who had been Agent Booth, the person secretly corresponding with him.

When Bea had instant-messaged him, suggesting that Mark Stone had faked being drunk, it dawned on Charlie. Just before Stone crashed into the boys with the shopping cart, he delivered what, at the time, sounded like a drunken bit of gibberish. But the words "elastic dreams" stuck in Charlie's mind.

And when the boy first considered Stone's actions as deliberate, those words came back to him, not as a delusional rant but as part of a purposeful act. And then those words "elastic dreams" had a new context and jangled another memory, one from the book of poetry left for him at the phone booth.

It was the only public reading of *April* that Marcus Rockman had ever done, and it was delivered for no other reason than its words had been so burned inside him that, in his time of need, they were the first things to bubble to the surface.

That they resonated with Charlie was a testament to the boy's devotion to his secret correspondent. Charlie had faithfully read the poems in *Word Silo*, not so much for a love of poetry but because they had been a gift from Agent Booth and therefore were important to him.

The boy had already viewed the book as a secret code to decipher, a jumble of clues that would lead him to a greater understanding. He thought it had been a greater understanding of himself, but he was about to revise that assumption.

"Elastic dreams," Charlie kept repeating to himself, as he scanned each poem, his confidence in his memory being shaken as he got deeper and deeper into the book without success.

But then he read *April*, and it all fit. Not just the words "elastic dreams" but the whole first stanza: the "weeds of time" part and "the life I never lived."

Charlie got goose bumps. He reached for the phone and called Bea.

"It's late, young man," Bishop Crumley said, answering the phone.

"I'm sorry, sir," Charlie said. "But it's important."

Bea was there then, shooing her father off the line.

"What did you find out?" she asked.

He told her.

"Read that poem again," she said.

And then the two teenagers broke new ground in the literary analysis of Marcus Rockman's work, reaching a level of understanding that had eluded a legion of graduate-level fine arts majors before them.

"April," Bea said. "I wonder who she is?"

"I don't know," Charlie said. "But I'll bet that's why he's homeless."

Charlie could hear Bishop Crumley interrupting Bea.

"Young lady," he said. "It's past your bedtime."

"But Daddy!" she said. "The homeless man on Belvedere is really a poet."

"That's nice," the bishop said, taking the phone out of his daughter's hand, then speaking into the receiver.

"Charlie Hope?"

"Yes, sir."

"The sleep of a laboring man is sweet. Ecclesiastes 5:12."

"Sir?"

"It's bedtime, boy."

When Pinky, Sindee and Santiago got to the hospital, they were told that visiting hours were over for the night.

"You can come back tomorrow morning," the man at the security desk said.

"But I'm his lawyer," Santiago said.

He was wearing a T-shirt with Che Guevara's likeness on it, frayed cutoffs and a ball cap that said "NAFTA sucks." The guard took one look at him and shook his head.

"Tomorrow morning," he said, before returning his attention to the little TV on his desk.

"C'mon," Sindee said to her friends. "Let's go get a drink."

But once outside, Santiago announced they were going to "use an alternate route" to Mark Stone's room.

"You're not going to let that fascist rent-a-cop stop us, are you?" he asked, as he led them through the emergency entrance and up to the room number Pinky had been given over the phone.

They slipped into Stone's room unnoticed. It was dark, and they could make out the shape of his body lying in the bed.

"Mark?" Santiago whispered. "Mark?"

Sindee turned on the light by the sink, then gasped at what she saw.

"Oh, no!" Pinky said.

Charlie Hope couldn't sleep. He stared at the ceiling of his room and tried to calm down. But it was no use.

He picked up the phone and called his mother. But he could hear her cellphone ringing in the kitchen, meaning she had forgotten to take it. So he got dressed and went down the hall to his sister's room.

"I'm going out for a while," he told her. "Mom will be home soon."

Luna sat up in bed.

"Where are you going?"

"Never mind."

"Did you tell Mom?"

He didn't answer.

"You're going to get in trouble," Luna said, but he was already out the front door with a flashlight in his hand.

He walked to Belvedere, keeping to the shadows and hoping he could make it back home before his mother returned from the hospital. The street was quiet now, except for the occasional passing car.

At the corner of Lake Avenue, the abandoned gas station was on a lot so dark that Charlie nearly lost his nerve. But he took a deep breath and turned on his flashlight as he snuck behind the gas station. He was invisible from Belvedere now as he played his light over the ground, looking for Mark Stone's belongings.

He saw the bicycle hidden near the garbage-bin enclosure behind the building, and the milk crate was there, too. But there were no other traces of Stone's life, as Charlie scanned the ground with the flashlight, walking slowly through the lot and into the alleyway.

He traced his way back to the rear of the gas station and was about to consider it a wasted trip when, in a final gesture, he pushed on the glass door at the rear of the station, fully expecting to find it locked. But the door swung open with his weight, and he stumbled forward into a gutted, dark room.

He trained the flashlight to one side of the room and stopped when it illuminated a mattress, a few books and a stack of papers in a folder. He saw instantly that the stack contained the weeks of messages he had left in the phone booth across the street. He crouched down and leafed through them. As he did, something fell out of the pile.

It was a newspaper obituary from three years ago.

Waverly, Celia, age 39, of Bay Shore, passed away Sunday . . .

Charlie read it quickly, scanning for a clue.

. . . attended St. Patrick's School . . .

He was so intent on reading it, he didn't hear the first sound that came from the other side of the dark room.

. . . survived by her daughter, April, age 20 . . .

Charlie was reading it for the second time before he realized that somebody else was in the room, and that somebody was walking toward him.

Charlie screamed, dropping the flashlight, which broke in pieces on the cement floor, and plunged the room in darkness. He tried to run to the door, but a pair of strong arms held him there.

24
Night moves

Charlie Hope struggled against the dark figure who held him, preventing the boy from reaching the door of the abandoned gas station. His blood was racing as he flailed at his unknown attacker in the darkness.

He didn't stop struggling until the voice of the man pierced through the alarm bells ringing in his head.

"Charlie, it's me. It's me, Charlie. It's me. Relax, Charlie. It's only me."

The boy peered through the darkness.

"Mark?"

"Yes."

Charlie moved away from the man's grip. "I thought you were in the hospital."

"I was," he said. "But I decided to check myself out tonight."

Charlie heard the man groan softly as he settled himself on the floor, somewhere in the dark room.

"I've found out some stuff about you," the boy said.

He couldn't see the man's reaction, so he pressed on.

"You're the person who has been leaving things for me in the phone booth across the street. Aren't you?"

Silence from across the room.

"And the other day, when Ray-Ray and those guys were about to beat me up, you weren't really drunk. You were just pretending so you could save me."

Charlie waited for an answer now.

"Is that it?" Mark said.

"No," Charlie said. "There's more. You're Marcus Rockman."

The boy waited for a moment. But there was no acknowledgment.

"Right?" Charlie said.

"Continue," Mark said.

"And that other day, when you were trying to save me, you recited a verse from your poem, *April*."

"I did?" Mark said, genuinely surprised.

"Who's April?"

Stone didn't answer.

"April is probably the same April that's in that newspaper story over there with your things," the boy said. "The daughter of that woman who died."

"Celia," Stone said.

"Yeah, that's the name," the boy said. "She your wife?"

"No," Stone said. "But April is our daughter."

"Where is April?"

"Charlie, if only you could tell me that, too."

They heard the sound of a car pulling up.

"Get down," Stone said.

Somebody was walking outside the abandoned station. Whoever it was, though, wasn't there for long. They listened as the car drove away.

"I'd better get back," Charlie said, "before my mother finds out I'm gone."

"It's nothing to be alarmed about," Santiago Klein told Sindee and Pinky as they stood in the hospital room, looking at the pillows and linens arranged to appear as a sleeping person in Mark Stone's hospital bed. "Mark is a free spirit. I'm sure he just decided to leave on his own."

"So I guess this means he's feeling better," Sindee said.

"Good enough to walk out of here," Klein said.

"Should we tell somebody?" Pinky said.

"We shouldn't even be up here," Sindee said.

"Let's just go," Klein said.

"For a drink," Sindee said. "Don't let me go back home so soon. I don't think I can face another shower yet."

And so they slipped out of the hospital and drove to Clematis Street, where they settled into a dark booth at O'Shea's Irish Pub and hoisted pints to the health of Mark Stone, wherever he might be.

Detective Carl LaCerda had started to take the burglaries in Pelican Park personally. The homeowners association had put pressure on Mayor Lois Frankel to do something, and that pressure, in the form of an expletive-filled rant, gradually filtered down to the police chief, then to him.

LaCerda had taped to his wall a street map of the neighborhood, marking each home break-in with a red pushpin. He stared at that map for hours, searching for a pattern but coming up with nothing. The burglaries seemed to be random, clearly the work of someone who knew the comings and goings of the people who lived there. The owners of the ransacked homes were sometimes out for only a few hours when the break-ins occurred.

They happened both day and night, and no one had ever reported any suspicious activity around any of the homes.

"Not kids," LaCerda told his lieutenant. "This is professional work. Not only clean getting in and out, but none of the stuff has been showing up in the pawn shops, either."

It had been more than a week since the last burglary, and LaCerda had a feeling that the burglar or burglars were about to strike again. It was rare that the neighborhood went this long without a new break-in.

So, for a second night, LaCerda, who was working the 4-to-midnight shift, parked his unmarked car under a burned-out streetlight and sat behind the wheel, quietly waiting and watching.

He sat there patiently for more than an hour, slumping down in his seat, his eyes alert and looking for something out of the ordinary. He had his windows cracked open so he could listen, too. And it was the sound he heard first.

A dark figure was crossing through the neighborhood, a single person on foot, sticking close to the shadows. The person was being quiet but not so quiet as to avoid stepping on a fallen branch that alerted LaCerda.

"Ho, ho," he said quietly to himself. "What have we here?"

He waited for the shadowy figure to get halfway down the block before he opened his car door and slipped out, patting his service revolver before following down the street.

■

"Can I use your phone?" Pinky said, after fruitlessly searching her purse. "I must have left mine at home."

"Who you calling?" Sindee asked, handing Pinky her cellphone.

"Maybe Travis will join us," Pinky said.

That first pint went down so effortlessly, and now she was filled with a new warmth, and although she hadn't made plans to see Travis tonight, she thought it might be a good idea. Especially since noticing that Sindee and Santiago were playing footsie under the table, and she was beginning to feel like a fifth wheel.

Pinky had asked Travis earlier if he wanted to meet them for a drink, but he said he was planning to go to sleep early because he felt a cold coming on. And he did sound kind of post-nasally snotty.

But by the second pint, Pinky didn't care.

"Come on, answer the phone," she begged, as it rang five times before Travis' answering machine kicked on. "Travis! Where are you? Come out and play, Travis."

She hung up and handed the phone back to Sindee.

"Not home?"

"Probably knocked out with a Nyquil," Pinky said, frowning.

■

Travis Plum had had his eye on Sindee Swift's house for a good couple of months. Of course, he had had his eye on practically every house in Pelican Park. And with the help of Pinky Mulligan, he had been in many of them, given license to walk around the properties without drawing any suspicion.

He was, after all, a good real-estate prospect.

He had never broken into the houses Pinky showed him. But he had, over time, broken into many of the nearby homes, always careful to get a rundown from Pinky on the neighbors.

"So, what do the next-door neighbors do?" he'd ask casually.

And Pinky would tell him, and in her explanation, he'd find out how many people lived there, whether there was a dog and generally what sort of schedule the household kept. He'd case a house for days before breaking in and always made it a point not to be too greedy.

Jewelry, cash, small portable electronics. Only the stuff his fence would gladly take. He never left a print, and that included muddy footprints. He varied his work schedule and knew from the start that even the most careful burglar had to be lucky.

He also knew that if he was good enough, he'd be doomed by his own success. That, eventually, the number of burglaries in the neighborhood would reach a critical mass and there would be too many eyes and ears on the alert, and then, despite his best precautions, he'd get caught.

He had gotten caught before, and he had no intention of doing any more state time at Glades Correctional Institute. And so he knew that his work in Pelican Park was nearly over. It had been a good run, and it would be a shame to ruin it.

It was nearly time to break up with Pinky Mulligan and move on to some other romance with some other lonely real-estate woman in some other neighborhood. Maybe he'd try Martin County next. Stuart must have a few Pinky Mulligans waiting for a guy like him to come along.

But first, there was this matter of Sindee Swift's house. From the time he had first come to Pinky's house, he was intrigued by her good friend, Sindee. Not only for the reasons that most men were intrigued by Sindee, but because she lived alone, didn't have pets and appeared to have expensive tastes.

Pinky was always circumspect about what Sindee did for a living, and Travis didn't press her about it, not as much as he gently asked about what sort of activities she and Sindee did together outside the house.

"Sindee has a way of making anything fun," Pinky said, "even a homeowners association meeting."

And so Travis Plum waited and watched. When the homeowners meeting came up again, he was able to glean everything he'd need to know: that the meeting was in another home in the neighborhood and that Pinky and Sindee were going to the meeting together and probably going out for a drink afterward.

"You could join us," Pinky told Travis.

The cold he was getting was a good excuse.

"Not tonight, love," he said.

Sindee's home would be his final conquest in Pelican Park. Then he would move on. It crossed his mind to wait until he felt better, but who knew when the next neighborhood association meeting would be? And besides, his own apartment's lease was ending. It was time to close the book on Pelican Park.

He waited 15 minutes after Sindee left for the meeting before expertly disabling her alarm and slipping in through her back door. He left the ski mask on his face, a little extra insurance in case somebody turned up unexpectedly.

He made a conscious effort not to rush, going room by room, ending up in Sindee's bedroom, which was lit by soft lights. He nearly turned them off. But the room had blackout shades, and it would be easier working with some light.

He put his flashlight down on the bed and went through her drawers, emptying all her clothes on the bed, searching with his gloved hands for any hidden jewelry boxes or cash hoards. She had expensive jewelry, and he took it all. He found her rainy-day cash envelope and her portable DVD player. He even took a few pairs of never-worn Victoria's Secret underwear — she had so many — as a present to his real girlfriend, the young legal secretary that Pinky had spotted him with at The Cheesecake Factory.

He was about to leave the room when he was overcome by the urge to sneeze. He raised his nose to try to stifle it. He was unsuccessful.

Ha-*choo!* Oh, that felt good. He wiped his nose with his forearm, and that's when he saw the pair of cameras suspended from the ceiling. Their two unblinking lenses stared back at him.

He whistled softly.

Finding a broom in the kitchen, he returned to the bedroom and smashed both cameras with the handle. Then he picked up his stolen loot and quietly left through the back door.

25

Internet dragnet

Cosmo Hope sat in his apartment watching ESPN and sharing a bag of pork rinds with Gomez the Chihuahua, not the best of dinners for either of them. As on many recent nights, he began to wonder what his ex-wife was up to.

Since their divorce and the near-romantic turn of events on the very night it became final, Cosmo had lived with the growing certainty that he had been a chump.

The dog settled into a sleeping position next to him and gave a big, asthmatic sigh before unleashing a silent blast of flatulence that propelled Cosmo from the couch, spilling beer down the front of his shirt.

"Gomez!" he shouted. "You're disgusting!"

He was up now, wiping off his shirt, which put him at the kitchen counter, which put him near the phone, which made him do something he told himself he would resist. Just one little call, just to chat.

He didn't think he could face getting back on the couch with the dog until the air had had a chance to clear. He called his ex-wife's number.

"Mulligan-Hope residence, Luna speaking."

"Luna, this is your dad."

"Hi, Daddy."

"What's this Mulligan-Hope nonsense?"

"I'm thinking about hyphenating my name."

"I didn't raise any hyphenated children."

"Like Catherine Zeta-Jones."

"Zeta's just her middle name."

"No, it's not."

"I didn't divorce you and Charlie, honey. I divorced your mommy."

"I thought she divorced you."

"No matter. The point is, you are a Hope."

"And a Mulligan."

Cosmo gave up.

"What are you doing?"

"Nothing."

"How was school today?"

"Bor-ring."

"Mommy there?"

"No. She went out."

"But it's nearly 10 o'clock."

"Mommy doesn't have a bedtime."

"Is she with that guy with the hair, Princess Valiant?"

He heard Luna laugh.

"She's with Sindee."

"Oh," Cosmo said.

He was relieved and more than a little intrigued. After he hung up, he brought the rest of the bag of pork rinds to his desk, opened another beer and turned on his computer. Just checking, he told himself, still curious about the extent of his ex-wife's friendship with the vixen next door.

He typed in *www.iseesultrysindee.com*, then his user name and password, and waited in anticipation for his virtual tour of Sindee's house. He clicked straight to the bedroom, where he half expected to see Sindee and his ex-wife, perhaps sitting on the edge of the bed, politely sipping a freshly chilled bottle of champagne.

Instead, he saw a figure in dark clothing hunched over Sindee's dresser.

It was a man. Cosmo couldn't see much of him, though. The man wore a ski cap that covered his head and most of his face. He had gloves on, too, and it didn't take long for Cosmo to see this wasn't one of Sindee's suitors. It was a burglar who was ransacking the contents of Sindee's bedroom, stealing her jewelry — and even her underwear.

Cosmo popped up from his chair.

"No!" he cried, wishing he could somehow burst through the screen and stop the desecration of this temple of lust.

And then he thought of his children, knowing that at this very moment, in the very next house from where they were, a criminal was at work. If he weren't a half-hour's drive from there, he'd already be in his truck, racing there to protect them and apprehend the thief.

"Think, think, think," he told himself, pacing around his kitchen.

He dialed his wife's house again.

"Mulligan-Hope residence, Luna speaking."

"Cupcake, it's Daddy again."

"I know who it is."

"Please, honey. Put Charlie on the phone."

"Um, why?"

"I don't have time to talk, Luna. Please. Just bring your brother to the phone."

"I'm going to be in middle school next year, Daddy. You don't have to treat me like a baby."

"Please, Luna. Just get your brother."

"I can't," she said.

"If this is all about being mad at me for . . ."

"I'm covering for him."

"What do you mean?"

"He's not home."

"Where did he go?"

"I'm covering for him. It's not polite to ask me too many questions. I don't want to be a snitch."

"Luna!"

"So how was work today, Daddy?"

"Luna! This is important!"

"I don't know. He didn't tell me. He just walked out with a flashlight in his hand."

Cosmo took a deep breath.

"OK, listen to me, honey. I want you to make sure all the doors in the house are locked real good. Do you understand?"

"Daddy, you sound weird."

"There's a burglar in the neighborhood."

"Aren't you in Boca?"

"Yes, honey, you need to . . ."

"So how do you know there's a burglar in Pelican Park?"

"Because . . . there's no time to explain."

"Are you psychic, Daddy?"

"Lock the doors, honey. I'm on my way up there."

Cosmo hung up and dialed 911.

"Sir, do you have an emergency?" a dispatcher said, answering the phone.

"Yes, I'd like to report a burglary in progress in West Palm Beach."

"Sir, this is Boca Raton dispatch."

"You're the police. I'm calling the police to report a crime."

"In another jurisdiction, sir."

"Does that make it not a crime?"

"Excuse me for asking, sir, but how do you know about a crime in progress in West Palm Beach when you're calling from a Boca Raton number?"

"Simple, I know because . . . never mind."

He hung up and asked for directory assistance for West Palm Beach, getting the non-emergency number for the city police department.

"Sir, is this an emergency?"

"Yes," he said.

"Then please dial 911."

"No, wait. It's not. I mean, it is. But I can't."

"Sir?"

"There's a burglary in progress at a home in Pelican Park. If you hurry, you can catch the guy."

"Do you have a view of the residence now, sir?"

"Um, no. I'm calling from Boca."

"Sir?"

"Please, there's no time to explain. You just need to hurry and get somebody there before he gets away."

He left the information with the dispatcher, not convinced at all that she had taken him for anything but a nut. Then he hopped in his pickup with Gomez and floored it to I-95, figuring he could make it to Pelican Park in 25 minutes.

Travis Plum was hoping those surveillance cameras in Sindee's house weren't working. But by the time he had crept stealthily back to his parked car on the next block, he already had a sense that something was wrong. As he pulled away from the curb with his lights off, he noticed what surely must be a detective's car parked on the next block. He reached down and flicked on the police scanner hidden under the dashboard.

A burglary-in-progress call was going out. Think fast, he told himself. There would be marked cars coming into the neighborhood, and they'd stop anyone driving out.

It was too risky to be on the move now. He'd have to come up with a plan.

He drove down the block and parked in the driveway of a dark house with a weed-strewn yard. The driveway was empty, and everything was in such a state of disrepair that it was clear the place was abandoned. He changed his clothes quickly in the car, wriggling out of his dark clothing and putting on a nice pair of slacks and a linen shirt.

He took all the clothes he had been wearing and threw them in a black plastic leaf bag, then walked quickly to the curb and tossed the bag on a pile of lawn debris on the swale of a nearby home.

He sat back in his car and waited. The first marked cruiser went down the street about two minutes later. His mind raced. What if he needed an alibi?

He picked up his cellphone and punched in Pinky's home number, surprised when her daughter answered.

"Daddy?"

"No, this is Travis."

"Oh, it's only you."

"Can I speak to your mom?"

"She's not here, and besides, there's a bunch of crime going on, so I can't talk."

"What's wrong?"

"Somebody's breaking into houses."

"No!"

"Yes. Daddy told me to lock all the doors. He's on his way."

It dawned on Travis. This would be perfect.

"I am too, honey. You just sit tight."

"But, but . . ."

He hung up.

He started to back out of the driveway. But there was one more thing he had to figure out.

He looked through the bag of items he had stolen. He hated to part with any of it, but safety called for a scapegoat here. So he picked out a couple of pieces of jewelry and drove at a leisurely pace, pulling behind the empty gas station at Lake and Belvedere. Travis carried the small satin bag of jewelry over to what seemed like a suitable hiding spot near the Dumpster.

Perfect. He drove to Pinky's, parked in her driveway and raced up the walkway, the picture of concern.

Across the way, two squad cars were parked in front of Sindee's house, and he could hear police radios squawking in the back yard.

"It's Travis!" he said, knocking on Pinky's door.

Luna opened it slowly, and he pushed the rest of the way in.

"Oh, you poor little girl," he said, patting her on the head. "You must be so frightened."

"I'm not little," Luna said. "And besides, the burglar's gone. There's just police there."

"Where's your mom?" he asked.

"Here she comes now," Luna said, as a car screeched up to the curb.

26

Bologna sandwich

"Uh-oh, my mother's back," Charlie Hope said, as they rounded the block and spotted her Lexus in front of the house.

"Are you going to be in trouble?" asked Mark Stone, who had insisted on walking Charlie home.

"Don't worry. I left my bedroom window open just in case something like this happened. As long as Luna didn't rat me out, I'll be fine."

So Charlie said goodbye to Stone and continued toward his house. It wasn't until the boy was nearly home that he noticed the two police cruisers in front of Sindee's house and Travis' BMW parked in his own driveway.

Charlie scrambled into the back yard and boosted himself into his bedroom. As he was nearly through the open window, he heard another vehicle pulling up to the house. He knew the sound of Cosmo's truck by heart.

What was his father doing here?

As Charlie tumbled into his room, he heard his dad running up the walkway with Gomez's asthmatic rumble bringing up the rear.

Then, groping around in the dark, Charlie found his bed, pulled down the covers and jumped in, not even bothering to take off his clothes. He closed his eyes, pretending to be asleep, waiting for the sound of his beaded curtains to part and the lights to go on. He didn't have to wait long.

■

Detective Carl LaCerda followed the shadowy figure through the neighborhood but found it hard to gain ground. Whoever he was following was walking too fast, obviously trying to get out of the neighborhood as quickly as possible. The detective had to break into a trot, breathing heavily now and unable to be as quiet as he wanted to be.

"Stop!" the detective shouted.

Instead, the man just ran. LaCerda picked up the pace and reached for his radio, turning it on as he ran.

"This is 706 . . . request assist from any unit in vicinity of Pelican Park . . . I'm in pursuit . . . on foot . . . white male subject . . ."

He continued, falling farther behind as he talked and growing more convinced that the person was getting away. Miraculously, a cruiser zoomed past LaCerda and pulled up next to the running man.

An officer popped out of the car, his gun already drawn, and the running man stopped in his tracks. A few seconds later, LaCerda, sweaty and out of breath, arrived. The officer already had the suspect spread-eagled against the squad car. The detective recognized the officer, Ed McGraner, as well as the man McGraner was patting down.

"Mark Stone," the detective said. "What brings you to Pelican Park tonight?"

"Walking."

"Looked like running to me."

"I didn't know I was being chased by a police officer."

"And you always go for these late-night walks through Pelican Park?"

"No."

McGraner finished patting down Stone.

"He's clean, Carl."

"Nice work getting here, Ed. That was fast."

"We're working a Signal 21 a couple of blocks away."

"Really?" LaCerda said. "Did you hear that, Stone?"

The man didn't answer.

"Here I think maybe you're just up to your usual peeping Tom stuff, but it turns out I might have to revise my opinion of you. Have you been breaking into houses tonight?"

"No," Stone said.

"Just out for a walk?"

Stone appeared ready to say something, but then just kept quiet.

■

When Pinky, Sindee and Santiago drove back to the neighborhood after their pints at O'Shea's, they were a little giddy. But their mood quickly changed when they rounded the corner and saw the squad cars.

"Tell me there aren't cops at my house," Sindee moaned.

Pinky was looking at the BMW in her driveway.

"What's Travis doing here?" she wondered.

They parked. Sindee and Santiago headed to Sindee's house, and Pinky raced to hers. She found Travis and Luna standing in the living room.

"Mommy!" Luna ran to her.

"Honey, what happened?"

It was Travis who answered.

"Apparently, there's been a break-in next-door, and when Luna told me you weren't home, I . . ."

"When did you talk to Luna?"

"I called about 20 minutes ago," Travis said. "I wanted to know if you'd meet me for a drink, but I see you already beat me to it."

"I thought you were nursing a cold."

"I am," he said, "but I missed you, hon. I know, it's selfish of me."

"Wait, wait," Pinky said. "I called you at home to ask you to meet us at O'Shea's, but you didn't answer."

Travis looked confused, Then his expression changed.

"Nuts," Travis said, looking dejected. "I must have absent-mindedly turned the ringer off on my phone again."

"Oh," Pinky said.

"When I called here, Luna told me there was a burglar on the loose and that you weren't home, so I came over as quickly as possible."

"Travis," Pinky said, going over to give him a hug. "Thanks for being so thoughtful."

Pinky looked down at Luna.

"Honey, everything will be OK. You need to get to bed now. Tomorrow's a school day."

"But I want to wait for Daddy," she said.

"Daddy?"

"And Charlie," Luna said, quickly clapping her hands over her mouth.

Pinky walked down the hall to her son's bedroom, parted the beaded curtains and saw Charlie's empty bed.

"Luna," she said, returning to the living room. "Would you mind telling me where your brother is?"

"I can't," her daughter answered. "I'm covering. Besides, he didn't say."

Pinky was already on the phone, dialing Bishop Crumley's number. He answered on the fourth ring, and she could tell she'd woken him up.

"Calvin, I'm sorry to bother you," she said. "But could you do me a favor? Is your daughter missing, by any chance?"

The next 10 minutes were a blur. People kept showing up at Pinky's house: police officers, Sindee and Santiago, Bishop Crumley, and finally her ex-husband and Gomez, who immediately began growling and snapping at Santiago Klein again.

"I can't help it," Cosmo was saying. "He doesn't like lawyers."

Pinky was getting ice, putting on coffee and fretting about her teenage son when her ex-husband walked up to her in the kitchen and said in a quiet voice, "Follow me."

"What is it, Cosmo?"

"C'mon," he said, pulling her along with him. "Did you happen to look for Charlie in his room?"

"Duh!"

"Well, you didn't look hard enough," Cosmo said.

He pushed back the beaded curtain and flipped on the light, and there was Charlie Hope, eyes closed, apparently asleep in his bed.

"Charles Michael Hope!" Pinky said.

Charlie stirred as if from a deep sleep, pretending the light was bothering his eyes.

"Mom? Dad? What's going on?"

"That's my question to you!" Pinky said.

"I'm sleeping," the boy said, rolling onto his side, away from her.

Pinky walked over to the bed and pulled down the covers in one swift motion, and there was Charlie, still in his clothes, right down to his Nike basketball shoes.

"Busted," Cosmo said.

"I can explain," Charlie said.

But that's when Luna came running into the bedroom.

"The police want to talk to everybody," she announced.

When Pinky returned to the living room, she saw there were two more cops than before. A sergeant named Benedict was writing things down.

"I think I already gave this information to one of the other officers," Sindee was saying.

"Yes, but I'm writing the official report, so I need to start from scratch here," Benedict said.

"It's Switzer, S-W-I-T-Z-E-R," Sindee said. "First name, Deloris."

"Deloris?" Luna said.

"Young lady, it's bedtime," Pinky said.

"But your name is Sindee," the girl said, ignoring her mother.

The sergeant paused with his pen.

"Sindee Swift is my . . . my business name," she said.

"And what sort of business is that, Deloris?" Benedict asked.

"Um, high tech," Sindee said.

Bishop Crumley sat down on the couch and erupted into Scripture.

"Watch and pray that ye enter not into temptation," the bishop said, readjusting his purple silk cleric's hat. "The spirit is indeed willing, but the flesh is weak. Matthew 26:41."

"Hike," Sindee said, glaring at the bishop, then returning her attention to the sergeant, who seemed hopelessly confused.

"And your employer is?" he asked.

"I'm self-employed," she said.

"Can I make you a bologna sandwich, Calvin?" Pinky asked the bishop.

"I'll have one," Cosmo said.

But nobody moved.

"Excuse me, sergeant. Is all this really necessary?" Santiago Klein asked.

The sergeant ignored Klein and pressed on.

"There are lots of surveillance cameras in your home, Ms. Switzer," Benedict said. "You must have been very concerned with security."

"I think everybody is concerned with security," Pinky said.

Travis, who was standing behind Pinky as she sat in a chair, patted her shoulders reassuringly. Cosmo glared at him.

Travis saw Cosmo staring at him and nodded calmly. Then he sneezed.

"Bless you," Pinky said, as Travis went to the kitchen to blow his nose.

Cosmo followed him there. Travis didn't notice Cosmo until he turned to throw out the napkin in the kitchen trash.

"How's the lawn business, Cosmo?"

Cosmo ignored the question. He was helping himself to a sandwich from the cold cuts in the refrigerator.

"Tell me something, Travis. Can't you find any single women — in your case, maybe somebody who can cut hair?"

"Pinky is not married anymore," Travis said, stiffly brushing past Cosmo to go back to the living room.

When he got there, the sergeant was talking.

"No, we don't have a description of the suspect," he was saying.

"But I thought you said you found out about the break-in from a burglary-in-progress call from a neighbor," Klein said.

"That's partially true. But the call wasn't from a neighbor," Benedict said. "It was actually from Boca Raton."

"Boca Raton?" Pinky said. "How would somebody in Boca Raton know there's a burglary going on in West Palm Beach?"

The sergeant was flipping through his notes.

"The caller wouldn't leave his name, but the number was traced to a phone listed under the name Cosmo Hope. Ring any bells?"

Cosmo walked back into the room, holding an enormous sandwich up to his mouth. He took a bite, ejecting a glob of mayonnaise onto his shirt. Everyone turned to look at him.

"What did I miss?" he asked.

The others seemed to be at a loss for words, except for Luna.

"We were getting to the part about your psychic powers, Daddy."

27
Knocks on the door

For a few seconds, nobody said anything. The news that some-body from Boca Raton had reported a burglary in progress at Sindee's West Palm Beach house was the first surprise, but not as much as learning that the caller was Pinky's ex-husband, Cosmo.

For Sgt. Benedict, there was a third surprise: that the man stand-ing near him with the bologna sandwich was the same man who had placed the call.

"Wait a second here, I'm confused," the police sergeant said. "You're Cosmo Hope?"

Cosmo swallowed and nodded. Then it dawned on Sindee.

"You're a member," she said, looking at Cosmo in a kind of amaze-ment that erupted from her as a spoken thought.

"A member?" the cop said.

"A *member!*" Pinky said, curling her lip in disgust as the full real-ization sunk in.

Sindee had already picked up a pillow on the couch and put it in front of her, as if it could somehow shield her past online nakedness from her best friend's ex.

"I'm lost here," Travis said.

Bishop Crumley looked at his watch.

"Everything seems to be under control," he said. "So I'm going back to bed."

But he didn't move. Cosmo bent down and fed the rest of his sand-wich to Gomez, taking the time to watch the dog gobble every last crumb. When he straightened up, everyone was still looking at him.

"Hey," he said. "Let's not get sidetracked here. The important thing is to find this burglar."

Nobody said anything, so Cosmo plowed on.

"White guy. Dark clothing. And a dark ski cap on his head. I couldn't get a good look at him. But that should be something to go on."

The sergeant was still frowning.

"Let's back up a bit," he said. "You're in Boca and . . ."

It was no use. Cosmo would just have to explain it all.

"OK, OK. It's like this," he began.

But he was spared by a knock at the door and the surprise entrance of Detective Carl LaCerda with news.

"I have a suspect in custody," the detective announced.

"That's great!" Cosmo said.

"It's that homeless guy who hangs out on Belvedere," the detective said.

"Whoa!" Santiago Klein said. "That's not possible."

LaCerda was barraged with complaints from Pinky, Sindee and Santiago, as they all started talking at once, telling LaCerda that Mark Stone had just been in the hospital and that there must be some mistake.

"Please, please," the detective said. "Calm down. There's no mistake. Take it from me, some people aren't who they seem to be."

That's when Charlie couldn't contain himself any longer. He had been listening to everything from his room, awaiting what would be certain punishment for sneaking out that night. But he couldn't be quiet now. He walked out into the middle of the living room and hushed the adults.

"You don't know him, either," he said, pointing an accusing finger at the detective.

"Charlie," his mother said, "be quiet."

"No, Mom. This is important. Mark Stone isn't a burglar. He's a poet."

"Charlie, I'm not going to tell you again," Pinky said.

"We caught him prowling the neighborhood," LaCerda said.

"He wasn't prowling the neighborhood," Charlie said. "He was walking me home. I went to see him. That's where I was tonight."

"What possible reason could you have to visit a homeless man?" his mother asked.

"He's my friend," Charlie said. "You don't know anything about him."

"I believe you," Santiago Klein said. "Detective, where are you holding my client?"

The detective turned, noticing for the first time that the guy in the Che Guevara shirt was that meddlesome public defender.

"Mr. Klein, what a pleasant surprise."

"You do not have my permission to speak with my client," Klein said.

"I don't remember Stone saying anything about requesting a lawyer."

"You don't know anything about him!" Charlie said. "His name isn't Mark Stone. It's Marcus Rockman."

Travis shook his head.

"Is this the homeless guy who cuts your lawn?" he asked Pinky. She nodded.

"There was something about him I just didn't trust," Travis said.

"What do you know?" Charlie said, turning to Travis.

"Charlie, that's enough," his mother said.

"He's a great poet. He was picked to be the poet laureate."

"He was?" Klein said. "That's amazing."

"Maybe a little too amazing," Travis said.

"What's a poet laureate?" Sindee asked.

"Unemployed," Travis said, before laughing at his own joke.

Charlie seemed to be on the edge of tears.

"Charlie," the detective said softly, "I'm going to say it again. I often find that people aren't who they seem to be."

Klein paced the floor.

"Don't patronize the boy, Carl," he said. "What's your probable cause? That a homeless man was walking through a neighborhood on the same night a house was burglarized? I hope you've got better than that."

LaCerda smiled.

"I do," he said. "That's why I stopped by here."

He reached into his jacket pocket and pulled out a clear plastic evidence bag, tossing it onto the coffee table.

"Any of this stuff look familiar?"

Sindee gasped.

"My jade bracelet," she said.

She leaned over, peering at the bag. "And that's my ring."

LaCerda asked: "Were these items taken during tonight's break-in?"

"They sure were," Sindee said.

"After Stone was stopped, we searched his spot on Belvedere and found them hidden in this black bag," LaCerda said, pulling the satin bag out of his pocket.

"That's mine, too," Sindee said.

Pinky looked pained. Charlie was incredulous.

"It can't be!" the boy was saying.

"It's true," the detective said.

"So, you didn't find any stolen items in my client's possession?"

Klein said.

"Mr. Klein, I just told you I did."

"No, you told me you found some stuff on Belvedere Road. But when you patted down Mr. Stone, as you most certainly did, you found nothing," the lawyer said.

"Save it for the courtroom, counselor," the detective said.

"Somebody else must have put that stolen stuff there," Charlie said.

LaCerda shook his head. Pinky sighed.

"And to think I let him mow my lawn," she said.

"Mom!"

"Please, go to bed, Charlie."

Travis reached over and put his arm around Pinky.

"There's no way you could have known, hon," he said, squeezing her.

Cosmo looked over at Travis consoling his wife, and for a few seconds, the two men's eyes met. Travis gave Cosmo a subtle, triumphant smile. But something suddenly twitched in Travis' face. It was the beginning impulse of a sneeze, something he tried to suppress but couldn't. His nose twitched a few times, then he lifted his head up, hoping to defuse the impulse. But he was unsuccessful.

Ha-*choo*.

"God bless you," Bishop Crumley said.

Travis nodded, then used his free forearm to casually swipe his face.

Cosmo stood transfixed. Something clicked with him. The sneeze and that motion. Thinking back to the burglar he had watched on his computer screen, he tried to remember everything about the person's appearance, but until now, he had forgotten about the sneeze.

But now everything clicked. The way the burglar first lifted his head, then sneezed, then made that motion with his arm.

The same one Travis had just made.

"Wait!" Cosmo shouted.

He hadn't said a peep since the embarrassing revelation of his computer voyeurism had become public knowledge. But now, The Lawn King had something to say, and in his imperial manner, he was going to say it loud and clear.

"Charlie is right! The homeless guy didn't do it!" Cosmo shouted.

He pointed a trembling, beefy finger at Travis.

"There's your burglar, detective!"

"What?" Pinky cried.

Travis laughed.

"Cosmo Hope, of all the despicable things you've done, this has to take the cake," Pinky spat out venomously.

"Pinky, your boyfriend is a crook."

Travis shook his head, the picture of disbelief.

"Cosmo, why do I get the feeling that this is an effort to deflect attention from your own perversity while also trying to undermine my personal life?" Pinky said.

"The way he just sneezed," Cosmo said. "That's the guy. It's what the guy on camera did."

"What guy on camera?" LaCerda said.

"I thought you said the burglar wore dark clothing," Sindee said.

"He did," Cosmo said.

Everyone looked at Travis, who had on a yellow, flowered Tommy Bahama shirt and khaki slacks. Travis looked down at his clothing and then met Cosmo's gaze.

"Oops," Travis said, and smiled.

Cosmo seemed flustered.

"He could have changed his clothes," Charlie said.

"Yeah, he could have changed," Cosmo said.

"I want to see my client," Klein said.

"Your client's an innocent man," Cosmo assured the lawyer.

But he could see doubt on the faces in the room, and when Travis shook his head again and gave Pinky's shoulder another squeeze, it was more than Cosmo could take.

He balled up his fists, and Pinky knew her ex-husband was seconds away from committing a felony in front of a room full of police officers.

"Cosmo, don't!"

He was halfway across the room, nearly to the point of no return, when he was saved, not by his wife's admonition, but by a knock on the front door.

Everyone froze. Even Cosmo.

Charlie, who was closest to the door, opened it.

Everyone turned to see an old man with wispy gray hair, thick black-rimmed eyeglasses and an undisguised mixture of timidity and fear on his face.

"Excuse me," he said, pausing for a moment to scan the faces in the room. "I believe all of you in this room know me."

There was an embarrassed silence as they all looked at each other, then back at the unfamiliar man at the door.

"We do?" Sindee said.

Then Bishop Crumley's eyes grew wide, and he gasped — the only person in the room to recognize the voice of this apparent stranger.

Everyone looked at the bishop for guidance. And he enlightened

them in his deep, sermonizing voice:
   "It's Uncle Sherman."

28
Uncle Sherman

Uncle Sherman, the man who had been heard but not seen in Pelican Park for years, was standing in Pinky's living room, as speechless as everyone else. Pinky finally spoke.

"Uh, please, Uncle Sherman, have a seat."

"I'd better not," he said. "I have to get back home."

"Yes, of course," she said, still wondering what powerful force had brought the neighborhood recluse out of his home on this night.

"Can somebody tell me what's going on here?" Detective LaCerda said.

Nobody answered.

"So you're Pinky Mulligan?" Uncle Sherman asked.

"Yes," she said, "and this is Sindee, and Santiago Klein, who lives on the next block, and I believe you know Bishop Crumley."

The bishop nodded to Uncle Sherman, a man he had until now only argued with through a speaker box at homeowners association meetings.

"You look smaller than your voice," Bishop Crumley said.

"Can't say the same about you," Uncle Sherman said.

He blinked a few times and scanned the other faces in the room.

"The Lawn King," he said, marveling at the sight of Cosmo. "I've seen your commercials."

"My children," Pinky said, by way of introduction, as Uncle Sherman's gaze traveled over to Charlie and Luna. "They're both on their way to bed."

Neither child moved.

"And this is my friend, Travis."

Travis smiled, but Uncle Sherman looked perplexed.

"Your friend?" he asked Pinky.

She nodded.

"Black BMW?" Uncle Sherman said. "The car that's parked in the driveway?"

"Sorry, she's not for sale," Travis said.

Uncle Sherman took off his glasses and rubbed the lenses.

"Excuse me for interrupting," LaCerda said, standing up and opening the front door for Uncle Sherman. "But we're in the middle of an investigation, sir. This isn't the time for a neighborhood chitchat."

Uncle Sherman looked pained.

"I'm not here to chitchat," he said. "I've come to help you in your investigation. You're LaCerda, right? The one who is 706."

It was LaCerda's turn to be confused.

"I listen to the scanner day and night," Uncle Sherman said. "I heard you tonight when you called for backup during a foot chase."

Sgt. Benedict got LaCerda's attention by clearing his throat.

"We've received tips from time to time from Uncle Sherman," the sergeant said. "He's one of the more devoted crime-watch people we have."

"Oh, hello, Sgt. Benedict," Uncle Sherman said. "I didn't see you there."

"OK," LaCerda said, starting to guide Uncle Sherman back out the front door. "If you leave me a phone number, Mr. . . . ."

"Soloway. But everybody calls me Uncle Sherman."

"I'll be sure to do so before I file my report."

LaCerda placed a hand on the little man's shoulder as he led him out the front door, then closed it.

"Now, where were we?" LaCerda said, walking back into the living room.

But before anyone could say a word, there was a knock on the door, and Uncle Sherman walked back in the house. LaCerda wasn't smiling this time.

"Wait a second, detective," Uncle Sherman said. "I haven't been out of my home in 10 years, so I wouldn't be here if I didn't have a very good reason."

When nobody said anything, Uncle Sherman continued.

"So, I was listening to the traffic about the burglary in the neighborhood. Naturally, I'm interested. I live two blocks away, and I make crime-watch reports to the Pelican Park Homeowners Association.

"Not long after the burglary call goes out, I hear a car park in my carport, which is empty because I don't have a car. I get food delivered, and there's really nothing else I need. If I do, neighbors just leave it at the door for me.

"I don't use many lights either, and I don't spend misguided energy on beautifying my yard, which frankly, has become a disturbing neighborhood obsession, if you ask me.

"I guess whoever parked in my carport thought nobody was living in my home. I went to the window and watched. The person sat in the car for a long while. I couldn't see very well. He was moving around a bit in the car.

"When he stepped out of the car, he had a garbage bag in his hand, which he threw on the pile of trash at a neighbor's yard. Then he got back in his car and drove away."

"Did you get the license plate of the car?" LaCerda asked.

"Yes, I did. Florida tag F78-KAS."

"Good, we can trace it."

"There's no need," Uncle Sherman said. "It's on that BMW in the driveway."

There was a moment of silence as Uncle Sherman stepped outside for a moment and returned with a black garbage bag in his hand.

"And here's the bag he threw on the curb."

LaCerda turned the bag upside-down, and before the first piece of clothing hit the floor, Cosmo Hope knew there would be a pair of dark pants, a dark shirt and a ski cap in the bag.

"Detective," Cosmo said. "I believe you've taken the wrong man into custody. Here's your burglar," he said, pointing to Travis.

"This is all nonsense," Travis said, doing his best impression of a man who has been outrageously accused of something he didn't do.

Pinky removed Travis' arm from around her shoulder and recoiled from him.

"Why am I such a fool when it comes to men!" she yelled, before standing up, crossing her arms and moving to the center of the room.

"Surely, you don't believe this crazy person," Travis said, looking beseechingly at Pinky, and then at LaCerda, who was bending over to inspect the clothes. "I'm being framed by a jealous husband and a senile old man."

"Did you get a good look at the person?" the detective asked Uncle Sherman.

"Like I said, it was dark, and my eyesight's not as good as it used to be. And unfortunately, I left my eyeglasses in the other room and didn't have them on."

"C'mon, this is ridiculous," Travis said.

"But I did go and get my binoculars in time to see the car pull away, and I got a good look at the license plate," Uncle Sherman said. "I wrote it down on this piece of paper."

He pulled a scrap of paper out of his pocket.

"Imagine my surprise when I saw the car in the driveway here," he said.

Travis held his palms up.

"This is almost too funny," he said. "Can we get back to reality?"

LaCerda stood up and looked at Uncle Sherman.

"You can't physically describe anything about this person you saw in the driveway?" LaCerda asked.

"No, not really," Uncle Sherman said.

"Approximate height? Facial hair? Clothing?"

Uncle Sherman shook his head.

"I'd like to know what sort of medication Uncle Sherman is on," Travis said, looking at the others, who avoided eye contact with him.

"Don't tell me you believe this nonsense!" Travis said, turning to the others, who stood silently around him.

Uncle Sherman was deep in thought.

"There was one thing," he said. "I don't know if this counts. I mean, it's nothing I saw. Like I said, I didn't have my glasses. But after he dumped the garbage bag and walked back up my driveway to the car, he paused for a second, and he sneezed."

Now, everyone in the room looked from Uncle Sherman to Travis.

"What? Is that supposed to be some, some . . ." Travis began, but he had to stop, because his nose started to twitch, and despite summoning up every ounce of his will, he couldn't prevent what was about to occur.

"Ha-*choo*."

Travis' sneeze made it impossible for Cosmo to contain himself.

"You son of a . . ." Cosmo said, lunging for him.

Pinky watched her ex-husband close the remaining distance to Travis, and this time, she stepped out of his way instead of trying to stop him.

■

An hour later, Travis left her house in handcuffs.

"No, I won't give you consent to search my car," he said. "This is nonsense. I want a lawyer. Pinky! Call an attorney for me! "

Instead, she walked into the kitchen, where her ex-husband was putting ice on his swollen knuckles. He looked down at her and smiled.

"That felt great," he said.

"Goodnight, Cosmo."

"Maybe Gomez and me could flop on the couch. It's kinda late to be driving back to Boca for . . ."

"No, I prefer you go now."

"Aren't you even going to say thanks?"

"Not tonight," she said.

"OK, OK," he said, dropping the ice bag in the sink.

Then he turned to her.

"You know I still love you," he said.

"And you have such an interesting way of showing it," she said.

He looked at her and saw she wasn't hopelessly angry at him, just mildly peeved — which gave him a reason to smile. And she nearly smiled back.

"Goodnight, Cosmo."

"Goodnight, Pinky."

After her ex-husband left, she put the coffee cups in the dishwasher and checked on her two kids, who were asleep in their rooms. When she went back into the living room, she discovered Jake Fisher, still in his waiter's garb, had arrived and was getting briefed on the night's events from Sindee.

"Oh, you poor dear," he said, rushing up to Pinky to give her a hug. "You all right?"

"I'll survive."

"I'm not sure I will," he said. "I hear I missed my chance to see Uncle Sherman."

Santiago Klein was talking to the detective.

"So you have no reason to detain my client," Santiago told LaCerda, who seemed to be looking for a reason.

"Where is he, Carl?" Pinky said.

"He's in custody," LaCerda said.

"For what?" Klein demanded. "You know he didn't do it."

"He may be a material witness," the detective said.

"Where in custody?" Pinky asked.

"He's in my car outside," the detective said.

"He's been outside all this time?" Pinky asked, racing for the door.

LaCerda's unmarked car was parked in front of Sindee's house. Pinky could see the silhouette of a person sitting in the back seat.

LaCerda, Santiago, Sindee and Jake followed her outside.

"Please let him go, Carl," Pinky begged. "You'll know where to find him if you need him. He's not going anywhere. You've already done your best to run him out of town."

LaCerda threw up his hands in surrender. He unlocked the car door and motioned for Mark Stone to get out.

The handcuffed homeless man blinked a few times, taking in the faces clustered near the car. Pinky saw resignation, rather than surprise, in Stone's expression.

LaCerda turned him around and removed the handcuffs.

"You're free to go," he told Stone. "But we'll be talking soon."

The detective got in his car and drove off. Stone stood there rubbing his wrists. Then he hung his head and started to shuffle away down the block.

"Wait," Pinky said, rushing after him and gently touching his arm. "Please come inside."

He turned to gaze from her face to the others and then toward Pinky's open front door.

29

The man who turned to Stone

Pinky Mulligan led Mark Stone to her kitchen, pulling out a seat for him at the table.

"I'll make us all a pot of tea," she said.

Sindee, Santiago and Jake took seats at the table, and although it was nearly 2 in the morning, nobody said a peep about needing to get home. There was an awkward silence as Pinky returned from the stove and sat down.

"Well," she said, trying to sound cheerful.

The homeless man stared down at his folded hands.

"Mark?" Santiago said. "We'd all like to help you."

Stone looked from face to face.

"I don't think you can," he said.

"Maybe we can help Marcus Rockman, then," Pinky said.

"Marcus Rockman," Stone said. "He's a fool."

"Tell us about him," Sindee said.

Stone took a deep breath.

"It's a long story."

The teapot whistled.

"We've got all night," Pinky said.

And so that's how it began, how Mark Stone unraveled the last three years of his life, starting from the day he got the surprise phone call in his campus office.

■

He didn't want to believe that the angry, uncouth person on the phone line could be his daughter. He told himself it was some kind of hoax, or maybe even an extortion attempt.

But then she read the letter he'd written to Celia Waverly, the one he'd sent from Dartmouth to explain why they would have to go their separate ways after graduation. He was under the impression his girlfriend had already had the abortion, and when she didn't respond to his letter, he had chalked it up to anger.

And in all the years since then, he never dwelled on the possibility that Celia Waverly might have given birth to their child and raised the baby without a father. It wasn't until he heard the angry voice of his daughter, some 20 years later, that it sank in that his life was far less tidy than he had imagined.

Celia had kept that college letter all those years, and now it had been passed down to the fruit of their doomed romance, a young woman who read it back to him with more dripping sarcasm than he could stand.

"Please," he said softly into the phone, "that's enough."

But she kept reading.

"The best thing for the both of us, Celia," she read, "is that we move on, continuing to grow and develop in our separate paths. I will always be grateful for the time we spent together and . . ."

"April," he interrupted. "I didn't know about you. I promise. Your mother never told me about you. If I had known . . ."

"Liar!"

"I didn't know."

"I watched her write to you. I sat across the kitchen table when she wrote you. I didn't even know who my father was. But that's when she told me. She said — I'll never forget her words — 'Your father is a great man, and he'll help us.'

"She knew where you were teaching. She had your stupid books. She even dragged me with her when you were doing a reading in San Francisco. I didn't know you were my father at the time. I was only 10. Never so bored in my life. When the reading was over, she made me walk up with her to get your stupid autograph on the book.

"I guess you didn't recognize her. The years weren't kind to Mom. But you didn't even look up. You wrote, 'To Celia — thanks for being a reader.' How brilliant!

"I think she must have wanted you to look at her and recognize her, and you just blew her off."

His mind raced back in time, trying to remember a signing at the City Lights bookstore, trying with all his might to recall a woman and a little girl there, but remembering only the slinky grad student who had spent the long weekend with him in the city.

"I'm sorry, April."

"So am I."

"I didn't know."

"I mailed the letter myself. I was 14. We waited a month. Never heard a word from you. My mother had this foolish idea that you would pay for the drug treatment program for me that she couldn't afford."

"Oh," he said, feeling as if he had just been punched in the stomach.

He remembered the letter now. He had walked home from campus, and it was sitting on a stack of mail on the kitchen counter. It had come during the final days of his brief marriage, and he had been too preoccupied, too sour to even be curious enough to open the letter. He tossed it in the trash unread, figuring it either had something to do with an offer to attend his high school reunion or to rekindle an old relationship — both unappealing offers at that time in his life.

"I'm sorry," he said. "Maybe I can make it up."

"Ha!"

It was a bitter laugh, followed by silence, the only sound on the phone line being that of passing traffic. He wondered whether the girl was crying. So he asked again:

"Is there something I can do now?"

"You're too late."

"It's never too late. Give me another chance to . . ."

"She's dead!"

His heart went cold.

"That's the only reason I'm calling. Because . . . because I don't think I should be . . . the only one . . . who cares."

"Where is she? I'll come. I'll drop everything."

He was talking fast now, already imagining himself trying to pick up the pieces. But the girl stopped him again with her bitter laugh.

"You're too late, again. She died about a month ago. They found her in her car, the engine running, parked in her garage. She didn't even leave a note."

"Why didn't you call sooner?"

"I didn't know until yesterday," she said bitterly. "I ran away from home when I was 16. I've been living on the street. You know what that's like, you pompous fool?"

"No, I don't."

"You ought to find out."

"How did you find out about your mother?"

"I'm in Florida. And when I got in trouble again, the probation officer tried calling my mother in New York, and that's how I found out she had died. Lovely, isn't it?"

Marcus Rockman knew that his own life was about to radically change.

"Let me help you, April."

"I don't need your help."

"Are you still in Florida? I'll fly there tomorrow. Or I'll fly you here. You can . . ."

And that's when she abruptly hung up the phone. Shaken, he sat there numbly for hours and penned his poem *April*.

Over the next few weeks, he canceled his classes, spending most of his time in his office, waiting for the phone to ring. She called back several times during those weeks, always collect and always — he would learn later — from the same pay phone in West Palm Beach.

But she always refused to let him help her. It seemed her only purpose in the calls was to inflict suffering and false hope on him.

"I'm coming to Florida," he finally told her. "Write this down. I've opened a post office box in West Palm Beach. You can always reach me there."

"How do you know I'm in West Palm Beach?"

He had hired a private investigator by then. He had turned down his appointment as poet laureate. Sold his home, given up his tenure.

At first, he lived at the Hotel Biba in West Palm Beach. He walked from the hotel to the corner of Lake and Belvedere, sitting across the street from the pay phone where she had made the calls.

"She's gone, man," the investigator told him. "All her old addresses are dead ends. She stopped showing up for probation, and she's not locked up, either. She could be anywhere."

"She's here," Rockman had said. "She's just making me suffer."

And he did. How many times had he run across Belvedere Road, convinced that the young women at the pay phone were his daughter.

"April?" he'd say hopefully.

But they always turned out to be dancers at the Kitten Club or neighborhood girls who thought he was trying to pick them up.

As time went on, he had a decision to make. Give up and go back to his old life, or dig in deeper. He chose the latter path.

He bought the abandoned gas station across the street from the phone booth and moved in.

He explained this journey to the people around the kitchen table. He had never verbalized any of this before, and in doing so, he felt more connected to the world than he had during the past three years.

"I knew she wouldn't let me see her as Marcus Rockman, so I thought by becoming Mark Stone and living on the street, as she had, I might break down that barrier," he said.

"But I never heard from her again. I check the post office box regularly and sit on the corner, day and night, looking across the street at that telephone booth. It's as if I've become frozen there."

Sindee dabbed tears.

"You still own that gas station?" Santiago asked.

"Yeah. I've been trespassing on my own property."

"Is there something we can do to help you?" Pinky asked.

"You already have," Stone said.

He told them about his friendship with Charlie and about their arrangement at the phone booth.

The group of friends refused to let Stone go back to the gas station. They invited him to their homes, but Pinky prevailed.

"You can be here when Charlie wakes up in the morning," she said. "It'll be a nice surprise for him."

After the others left, she opened the hide-a-bed in the living room.

"Help me put some fresh sheets on it," she said.

She and Mark Stone stood there on opposite sides of the thin mattress, tucking in the fitted sheet.

"I saw you that day," he said, not looking up. "When you helped the man in the wheelchair."

She looked up at him, surprised.

"In a way, that was the beginning for me," he said. "I had been numb before then, but seeing you do that was the first time I felt something in a long time."

She stopped tucking in the sheet.

"I tried to return the wheelchair, but it didn't work out," he said. "But that was the beginning."

"That was the beginning for me, too," she said. "That was the day I started reinventing myself."

The bed was made now. They stared at each other for a moment, then Pinky started out of the room. But she stopped halfway, turning toward him.

"When we talk in the morning, what should I call you?" she asked.

"What do you mean?"

"I'm just wondering if you'll still be Mark Stone when you wake up?"

"Yeah," he said. "I'm wondering about that, too."

30
A poem for Pelican Park

Since that night when so much was revealed at Pinky Mulligan's house, the plight of Mark Stone became a focus, not only in her life but in the lives of her children, and her friends and neighbors.

They invited him to dinner at their homes, and when he turned them down, as he always did, they delivered hot meals to him at the gas station.

Detective Carl LaCerda, once on a mission to run Mark Stone out of town, was now constantly asked by Pelican Park residents why he couldn't help find the man's lost daughter.

"I'm paid to solve crimes, not run a lost-and-found service," LaCerda complained.

But there weren't many crimes to solve in Pelican Park following the arrest of Travis Plum, who turned out to be Travis Winters, a career con artist.

Pinky showed up in court at his sentencing hearing to be there for Sindee, who had to attend because she was the victim in the case.

Rather than go to trial on a slew of felonies, Travis pleaded guilty to a single charge in hopes of spending less time in prison. The judge sentenced him to five years.

Santiago Klein dropped by, too, sitting with the women and whispering, "This is the first time I've ever rooted for the prosecution at sentencing hearing."

Klein left as soon as the judge announced the sentence. Pinky and Sindee lingered, watching as a bailiff rolled Travis' fingertips, one by one, in the ink to make his booking prints. He glanced over at the women, tossing his blond mane back with a flick of his head and blowing a kiss.

"I really know how to pick 'em, don't I?" Pinky whispered to Sindee while scowling in Travis' direction.

They sat there until Travis was handcuffed and escorted out a side door.

"It's a good thing he pled guilty," Sindee said. "I don't think they could have gotten Uncle Sherman out of his house to testify."

Uncle Sherman had returned to his reclusive life, existing once again as the disembodied voice on the speakerphone during Pelican Park Homeowners Association meetings. No one had seen him following that night at Pinky's house, and his appearance had gradually grown into a kind of neighborhood legend, embellished with clear disregard for the facts.

In some tellings, Uncle Sherman was a kind of grotesque crime-watch Elephant Man, who appeared with a bag over his head and walked with a limp. In other versions, he was as dashing as Paul Newman.

"Let's go for a drink to celebrate the incarceration of your boy-friend," Sindee told Pinky as they left the courthouse.

"I can't," Pinky said, glancing at her watch. "I've got to be heading home."

She didn't say why. But she had made a habit of being home when Mark Stone arrived to mow her lawn, a job he still held.

"You can invite Mark over," she had told her son, Charlie, who saw Stone nearly every day at the gas station, sometimes spending hours at a time.

"He's shy," Charlie had said. "I think he likes it best when I see him there."

Stone continued to help Charlie with his homework, but it was clear they had struck up a mutually important friendship, a source of both satisfaction and a little bit of envy for Charlie's mother.

On the days when Stone mowed her lawn, Pinky found herself making excuses to stay home and insisting he take a break in the middle of his duties to have tea and cookies with her.

It was on one of those crisp winter afternoons when she asked him for a favor. It was something she had wanted to do for weeks but wasn't sure if she had the nerve.

"Could you write me a poem?"

"A poem."

"Not for me, actually. But for the neighborhood."

Since joining the Pelican Park Homeowners Association, Pinky was convinced that the neighborhood needed more than a motto and designer lampposts to distinguish it from other city neighborhoods.

"We have these low walls at the entrances to the community. I'm sure you've seen them," Pinky said. "They're big enough for a four-line poem."

Mark Stone looked away.

"We'll pay you, of course."

"It's not that," he said. "It's just . . . I don't know if I can write again."

"Maybe it's time to find out."

And that had been the beginning of Mark Stone's real transformation into his former self, Marcus Rockman. Pinky stopped by the gas station the next day and gave him a pad of paper and some pens and pencils.

The next time he mowed her lawn, he reached into his pocket and handed her a folded piece of paper.

"Don't feel like you have to use it," he said. "If you don't like it . . ."

But she was already reading his meticulous printing:

More than wood, glass and stone
More than lawns and trees for shade
Homes, not houses, in Pelican Park
Where the best of dreams are made

"It's a little sappy," he said. "I could rework it a bit by . . ."

"It's perfect," Pinky said, looking up. "And what's wrong with a little sappy, anyway?"

The poem on the entry walls to Pelican Park created a stir, due largely to Jake Fisher, who happened to be a waiter for a table of *Palm Beach Post* reporters one night.

"I have a great human-interest story for you," he said.

A week later, the newspaper ran a story about how Marcus Rockman, America's most mysterious poet, had turned up homeless in West Palm Beach and was now plying his trade for a homeowners association.

Stone didn't pay much attention to the fuss. But he had started writing again, turning out poems he kept in an empty Krispy Kreme doughnuts box.

"Is the homeless man going to be your next boyfriend?" Luna asked her mother one morning over breakfast.

"Excuse me?" Pinky said, feigning shock at her daughter.

"It's just that, you know, if so, maybe you ought to find him a house," she said, stirring her spoon aimlessly through a pool of the pink milk left by her Froot Loops.

"Brush your teeth," Pinky said. "You're going to be late for school."

Luna ignored her.

"I mean, you're in the home business, and he's in the homeless business," the girl said. "Makes sense."

■

Three weeks later, Pinky Mulligan drove to the abandoned gas station, opening the passenger-side door and calling out, "Mark, get in."

She had never driven him in her car before.

"What's the matter?" he said, coming over to the car.

"Just get in," she said, patting the passenger seat. "I want to show you something."

She drove to a two-bedroom, cottage-style home just three blocks from her own house and parked in the driveway.

"Come on," she said, taking a key from her pocket and leading him toward the empty house.

"It's a new listing," she said. "But I'm not even putting my sign out front because I think I already have a buyer."

Mark Stone looked away.

"Who's that?" he said, pretending not to catch her drift.

"There's great potential here, Mark."

She opened the door, and they went inside.

He kept moving, stopping only to look out each window, standing there to gaze through the glass as if looking for someone.

"She'll find you if she wants to," Pinky finally said. "And when she does, at least you'll have something to offer her."

Pinky stood next to him.

"It's time, Mark. You need a home."

He turned to face her, and she could see the pain in his eyes. But something else was there, too, this time. He gently put his hand on her shoulder, the first time he had touched her. And they stood like that, the two of them, studying each other, neither one moving.

■

Two months later, America's would-be poet laureate sold the gas station property he owned on Belvedere Road and, in a simultaneous closing, bought the small house in Pelican Park.

Pinky bumped into Marvin Mallow in the title office later that day.

"What are you doing here?" he asked.

"What do you think, Marvin?"

Marvin Mallow had given up trying to scare her.

"Sold another one in Pelican Park?"

"You bet."

"You know, I'm thinking of moving north. Stuart. Palm City. St. Lucie. That's where the growth is," Marvin said.

Pinky tried not to smile.

She might have savored the moment a little more except that her cellphone was chirping.

"Hello?"

The mother of a boy at Charlie's school sounded frantic.

"What's going on at the school?" the woman was saying. "I just pulled up, and there's cop cars everywhere, two TV news trucks outside, and I saw police take away a boy in handcuffs."

Pinky ran to her car and raced toward the school, hyperventilating until she saw her son and Bea and Terrell Crumley walking home as they always did.

She pulled up to the curb, and they climbed in.

"What happened?" she asked.

"Ray-Ray finally screwed himself big time," Terrell said.

"Who's Ray-Ray?" Pinky asked.

"The boy who stabbed Mark Stone," Charlie said.

"Oh, no. Please, don't tell me that boy is still in school."

"Not anymore," Terrell said.

"What did he do?" Pinky asked. "Stab another kid?"

"Worse," Bea said.

"Worse?"

"Yeah," Charlie said. "He disrupted the FCAT."

■

Buoyed by his success in getting news coverage about Marcus Rockman's return to the world, Jake Fisher set out next to get him a poetry reading at the Barnes & Noble at CityPlace.

"We'll pack the place," Fisher told the bookstore's marketing director. "C'mon, we're not talking about some hack here. The man is practically the John Grisham of the iambic pentameter."

She looked at him dubiously.

"OK, so I don't know what I'm talking about," he said. "But I do know we'll all show up and buy coffee. I'll send a flier out to the whole neighborhood."

Coffee, Jake told his partner, Craig, is really what bookstores are about these days. It doesn't matter how the books sell, as long as people come in to sip $4 cups of coffee.

And so, on a summer Tuesday evening, Marcus Rockman held his first poetry reading in years.

At first, he declined the invitation. But his newfound neighborhood friends kept asking him to reconsider, and the truth was, he had started writing again in that little house of his. And it wouldn't be bad to air some of it out.

So he said he'd do it.

"I'll pick you up at 6:45," Pinky said.

"You don't have to," he told her. "I'll just ride my bike."

"Nonsense," she said. "What if it rains?"

So he let her pick him up, and he waited downstairs in the store until the marketing director told him it was time to begin.

He took a deep breath, walked to the store's escalator and rode up alone.

As he crested the second floor, he saw the table that had been set up for him, holding a stack of several of his titles. He saw the cordless microphone and the small amplifier. And he heard the whirring of the blender in the coffee shop, which was where he'd be talking, reading and signing.

He walked toward the spot, seeing a few dozen familiar faces turn to him: Santiago. Sindee. Jake and Craig. Bishop Crumley. Charlie and Luna. Bea and Terrell. Pinky. A bunch of other Pelican Park residents he had come to know by sight but not by name yet. And a sampling of the choir from The Holy Blood of the Everlasting Redeemer Church. Even Detective LaCerda was there. And, as Marcus Rockman walked toward them with his Krispy Kreme box full of unpublished poems under his arm, they rose as one and applauded.

He felt his face grow hot, and his eyes well with a new kind of tears. He cleared his throat, which had grown suddenly thick, and picked up the microphone with fingers that trembled.

"When I came to West Palm Beach three years ago, I never felt more alone, more isolated from the rest of the world," he said, his voice warbling and barely under control. "I don't feel like that now."

He read his poems for nearly an hour. Some were old, but most of them were new. Then he sat down, drained with a sense of catharsis and relief, and ready to sign books for the line of people that formed in front of him.

"You don't have to," he kept saying, as neighbor after neighbor appeared to buy one of his books.

"I want to," they'd say.

"Thank you," he told them, scribbling inscriptions, over and over again.

They walked away, one by one, leaving him there to sign for a few stragglers. Pinky, whose kids left with Bishop Crumley, waited behind to drive the poet home. The marketing director had asked him to sign some store copies and stood there, handing him books opened to the page he was to sign.

Pinky wandered off to the music section while he signed the remainder of the leftover books, and it wasn't until she was there that she noticed another straggler.

The woman was standing in the magazine aisles, which were adjacent to the coffee shop. Pinky had noticed her once during the reading. She wasn't part of the group that had come to listen to Marcus. But she had stood there within earshot, browsing through magazines with a few other people and showing no apparent interest in the author.

But now, those other people were gone, and she was still there. Pinky studied her and noticed how her eyes kept darting up from the magazines to the poet signing the books.

"Marcus!" Pinky shouted, unable to contain herself.

He looked over at Pinky, surprised by the alarm in her voice. And then he followed Pinky's eyes to the young woman in the magazine section.

How many times had Mark Stone looked at young women like her? How many times had he wondered to himself, "Could you be the one?" How many times had he allowed himself to imagine that his daughter had come looking for him?

Many times — but not too many times to imagine it again.

The woman had hollow, bloodshot eyes, dirty uncombed hair and a scar on her cheek. But what Marcus Rockman noticed most was that her upper lip was trembling slightly, and her chin was so much like her mother's.

He dumped the books back into the arms of the marketing director, who seemed confused.

"You haven't autographed these yet," she said.

But Marcus didn't hear her. He was standing, facing that young woman in the periodicals section, who, at that moment, was the only other person in the room.

"There was one poem I didn't read tonight," he called out to her. "I was saving it. I didn't know you were here."

And then he recited *April*, a poem he knew by heart — or more precisely, by broken heart.

"My regrets come to me in elastic dreams," he began, "in memories long covered by the weeds of time."

And as he did, she started towards to him, as if his words were tethered to an invisible line that reeled her in.

■

Pinky went down the escalator and out of the store. She needed air, and Marcus and his daughter needed to be alone for whatever was to be said or done.

She made her way to the central fountain at CityPlace, which was shooting streams of water high into the air to classical melodies. It was a lovely night to be outside. There was a breeze, which caused the fountain to fill the air with a fine mist. Heat lightning danced on the horizon, and couples were taking up most of the umbrella tables, huddled over cups of gelato.

She sat on the ledge of the fountain and sighed. She wasn't there long before she sensed somebody sitting next to her.

"There you are," he said.

The Lawn King had a fresh haircut but wore a shirt she still knew well enough to be able, even if blindfolded, to pinpoint its three major stains within a centimeter of their locations.

"Cosmo, what are you doing here?"

"I've come to listen to your landscaper recite poetry."

"You missed it. He started at 7."

"Luna told me 8," he said.

"I doubt it."

"Oh, shucks."

"Too late. As usual."

"I don't know," he said. "Seems to me I'm right on time. Want one of those Italian puddings?"

"Gelato," she said. "No thanks."

"So what are you doing out here?"

"Sitting."

"Waiting for the homeless guy?"

"He's not homeless anymore."

"Too bad," Cosmo said. "It would have been a good gimmick: Will Recite Poetry for Food."

She looked at him and shook her head.

"You're pathetic," she said.

"It's crossed my mind," he said.

They sat in silence for a while, allowing the mist to fall on them, staring off in different directions.

"Don't you have someplace to go?" she finally asked him.

"I'm already there."

They sat for another minute without talking.

"Cosmo?"

"Yes?"

She took a deep breath.

"If the offer still stands, I'll have that gelato."

"Good. Good. So will I."

He got up and headed toward Bacio. But after a few paces, he stopped and turned, happy to see her looking his way.

He walked back to her.

"I forgot to ask," he said. "What flavor?"

Pinky thought about it for a moment before arriving at her answer.

"Surprise me."

She looked at him again as he walked toward the gelato shop. Then she looked the other way to the door of the bookstore. But mostly, she just looked up.

Pinky Mulligan searched with all her might for stars, which she knew were up there, somewhere beyond the artificial light that rendered them, for now, invisible.

Praise for 'Pelican Park'

"I should have known better than to have makeup on before reading the final chapters of *Pelican Park*, which, at its emotional climax, had tears in my eyes and caused my makeup to run."

— Cynthia MacGregor

"I have been addicted to each and every one of your stories. And this time, I got my French Canadian friend involved, too. Julie is a lovely lady whose English isn't really good, but she loved reading *Pelican Park*. You are helping her English greatly, as well as providing her with lots of enjoyment."

— Ginger Horn

"Can we expect a sequel to *Pelican Park*? Don't leave us hanging . . . Do Pinky and Cosmo get together or not? What about Mark Stone and his relationship to Charlie? Does Uncle Sherman ever come out again? These are things we need to know."

— Betty Holland

"I awaited your recent serialized story with eager anticipation at the joy that I knew would be mine each day. The conclusion arrived much too quickly. But I guess that's what they say, 'Always leave 'em wanting more.' "

— Bruce Rosenfelder

"*Pelican Park* is a wonderful bit of nonsense . . . As a sometimes resident (snowbird) of a similar neighborhood here in West Palm Beach — perhaps even one that has give you some inspiration — you are right on."

— Lee Ecklund

"I'm hooked. I love it. I want more of it!

"Need any story ideas? I have lived in this area my whole life, and I frequent all the places you have mentioned. Keep up the good work. It gives me a reason to get out of bed in the morning."

— Joy Henderson

"I laughed, I cried, I fell in love with them all. I already have hopes and dreams for Pinky, and for Mark, and I want to work for Santiago."

— Elisabeth Hoffman

"Thanks for writing such a great book. I looked forward to reading *Pelican Park* every morning in the newspaper. Write another!!!"

— Lori Harper